TRANSCENDENCE

TRANSCENDENCE

Book Two of the Narrator Cycle

Ian Patterson

Book Cover & Illustration by Barış Şehri: https://baris.editionstilemizon.com/

Editing by Melinda Crouchley: https://www.melindacrouchley.com/

Paperback ISBN: 979-8-9909170-2-6

eBook ISBN: 979-8-9909170-3-3

— First published edition, 2025 —

To my wife, Angela. You're my always alpha-reader, plot-hole-pointer-outer, constant cheerleader, and the rock that my foundation is built on. Without you, none of this is possible. To my daughter, Indigo. You're my reminder that the future is still full of hope. You keep me forever young.

Don't be
blue

Drink
Indigo!

Try the
revolutionary
tonic
of youth!*

*No money? No problem! Long-term
work contracts available today for
those who can't pay.

*Life is like a game of cards. The hand that is dealt
you is determinism; the way you play it is free will.*

-Jawaharlal Nehru

*Every portrait that is painted with feeling is a
portrait of the artist, not of the sitter. The sitter is
merely the accident, the occasion. It is not he who
is revealed by the painter; it is rather the painter
who, on the coloured canvas, reveals himself.*

-Oscar Wilde, The Picture of Dorian Gray

ONE

NICHOLAS

In painted purples, reds, and whites, my world is colored by distant stars and galaxies. I see them, but exist somewhere separate, somewhere beyond them. The Cosmos, a transparent plain filled with antique doors that extends across every horizon. They connect to nothing, standing alone in their frames, but through each door is a new place, a new city.

Or, that's how it should be. I've spent weeks here, my only concept of time marked by my own muted footfalls, and every door I've opened is just a portal to glittering blackness. To another graveyard seed ship that never made it to a planet and floats in the vastness of space. Sometimes, from the view inside the door, I can see the breach in the walls of the city that was the final death note. Sometimes, there is nothing but floating debris.

I know that if I stepped through, I'd die in seconds. As a test, I put my hand through the first door I opened, and pulled it back immediately in excruciating pain. In a flash, it had swollen in the low vacuum and started to freeze. I wonder if anyone was alive when the end came to these places—the suffering would have been immense.

I follow my path through the Cosmos, a mostly translucent shape that shows everywhere my body has been, and will be. I think this is the map the Narrator gave me, but I don't understand how it works. I've tried to deviate from it, jumping to the side to break from its grasp, only to find that the path had always bent in the same way.

In the first days, I was obsessed with trying to understand what it meant. *Is this destiny? Who built this path, what's its function? Am I in control of where I head? Am I in control at all?* It's a strange thing to know where you'll head, to know what steps you'll take, and I can't tell if I'm actively choosing to trace them, or being propelled along them. The outcome is the same. I follow the guide to each new door, an endless stream of dead places.

The path I'm on presents one option, but there have to be others. There seem to be hundreds or even thousands of doors, so if all routes were possible between them, there would be millions of different paths. I stare down at the key etched in my palm, a parting gift from the Narrator that let us access this place, and for a moment it flashes in pain and seems to glow. Around me, the Cosmos pulses with the pain, temporarily showing me a complex network of potential paths. *Dotty is on one of those, she's following a different trajectory.*

Has Dotty found anything different? Is she safe? My thoughts have been dragged back to her constantly since we split. I replay that final argument in my head and watch as she walks away from me. Some days, I rage against her in my mind, angry at her lack of human compassion, and some days, I regret saying anything. I miss her deeply, and I don't know how much of it is missing human contact and how much is something more—something unresolved.

Charon rubs his head against my thigh, and it breaks me from my reverie. I realize I've been standing in front of another door for minutes, thinking. This has happened more and more the longer we've been here. I'm aware that it's probably a bad sign of dissociating from reality, but I can't seem to stop it. It's like I'm sleepwalking and when I snap back to the present, I'm somewhere new.

I scratch the top of Charon's head, and behind his ears, and a deep purr starts in his belly. He looks up to me in satisfaction, and I smile back to him. Thankfully our hunger and thirst seems to not feel the passing of time in this place, or he probably would've eaten me by now.

I reach out and open the door in front of me. Behind it is another dark room, no lights or signs of life. I sigh, and start to look closely through the door to find evidence of a hull breach, that inky void of final judgment. I'm bent down and trying to peer through the top of the frame, when a flash darts across my vision. I catch sight of someone running from the room on the other side of the door. My heart pounds and I fall backward. I hurriedly scramble to my feet and, without thinking, plunge through the door after the flash.

The air temperature shifts as I enter the new space. The Cosmos is hot, nearly body temperature, but here there is a chill to the air. Our city never felt this cold, even during simulated rain. I put that thought to the back of my mind and quickly assess the room. It's the same layout as the observatory in our city, but here it's dead. No sun or stars stream in through the window, the control panels show no blinking lights, and there's no hum of electricity.

The patter of bare feet running on metal flooring reaches me from somewhere in front, but the steps are growing distant now. I tear out of the observatory after them. I pass through the cleaning room that adjoins it, all of the mechanical arms hang down limply from the ceiling now. Charon joins me at my side, tentatively sniffing the air. I nearly freeze at the entrance to where Cerberus lived in my city, but in this one it's just a giant, empty hall.

In a streak of white, someone slips through the far door. They're half my size, a child maybe. I race after them, excitement building in me at finally seeing another living thing.

My eyes have adjusted to the darkness, and I notice now that there is the barest of light covering everything. A meek glow comes from fixtures set in the ceiling and walls, it softly breaks the darkness. I gain the other side of the great hall as Charon races behind me, and we go through the door. The anteroom has access to an elevator, its door slightly ajar at a strange angle, and to another mechanical door that moves slightly on hidden hinges. I rush to it, and find a set of service stairs extending into the blackness below. The sound of footfalls slapping against the metal steps echoes up, and I race down after them.

It's like my time in the Cosmos held my body in stasis. My conditioning is still strong as Charon and I race down flight after flight. He's faster than I am, but can't turn well on the flooring and keeps crashing into the walls. The stairwell seems to stretch infinitely, spiraling down every full turn to a new landing and a new door, each looking the exact same. I remember the height of the Medical Authority tower in my city, there's no way I can keep this pace until the bottom.

The slapping sound of my own feet and the crashing of Charon quickly blends with the echo of whoever we chase until it's all around me. I can't tell if they're above me or below me, and I feel half blind in the near dark.

With my chest and legs burning, I finally stop for a breath. I lean against a wall, panting, and listen as the cascading echoes dissipate. Whoever I was chasing, they're gone now, or not moving. *Did I pass them on the stairs?* I breathe, and think. The desire to see another human being was so overwhelming that I hadn't even paused to think why I was chasing them. *I've probably terrified them, what the hell is wrong with me?* Before this moment, I hadn't realized how lonely the past weeks had made me.

Somewhere below me, I hear a quiet groan of corroded door hinges. Instead of running after it, Charon and I make our way down slowly, quietly. Ten landings further I find the bottom of the service stairs, the door is left slightly ajar. I pull the door open slowly, and the same quiet groan fills the air, but I barely hear it. I'm too focused on what's on the other side of the door.

The sight of a Sun Gate so like my own stretches before me, bathed in soft backup lighting. But instead of glistening gold and bustling industry, the buildings are full of yawning holes that I can only see as the absence of light. Huge debris lines the walk; giant pieces of shrapnel let loose from buildings are pushed haphazardly into piles. Looking out over the other areas of the city in the distance, I see the jagged lines of broken skyscrapers. They stand like rows of chipped teeth all around me. In the soft glow that comes from the walls, so unlike the blinding daylight of my own city, there are holes that must nearly pierce the hull of the city.

The door I opened exits onto the perimeter of the park that I once saw with Dotty in my own city. It stretches to either side of me, with rolling hills that gradually decrease in elevation down to the entrance to Sun Gate. The great gate that once only let me through with Dotty's permission is blasted apart, split open. The park is lined with rows of stumps that were once trees, and there's a congregation of people sleeping outside. Maybe a hundred huddle around small fires at the periphery of a huge, ragged mass. In the flickering lights, I watch them go to the central pile occasionally and then return to their fires. The smell of burning wood, so foreign in my own city, drifts up to me.

What the hell happened here? What have these people lived through?

From what I can tell, the layout of our cities must be the same, like different models of the same thing. I think back to what the Narrator said, about how many cities he's seen end, and wonder what devil killed this one. And how long it's been dead. There's no sign of Inquisitors anywhere, no sign of light elsewhere in the city that I can see from this vantage.

The thrill I saw at seeing another person has quickly morphed to dread at finding this horror, this destruction. I want to turn and run back to the Cosmos, back to the safety of my loneliness.

But as soon as I think this, my feet turn toward the park, guided by some unseen hand—down to the fires. Something drives me, some need to know what happened, like finding a corpse and being insatiably curious as to how it died.

My boots find the grass, and from the crunching I can tell it's dead. *Doesn't it rain here anymore, or was it the lack of light?* I make it to the outer ring of stumps. From the door I saw they lined the entire park, but up close their true size shocks me. Each is colossal, nearly half my height in diameter. I bend down to touch one and find it a dried husk. It's been dead so long that there's no wood smell from it, no sap comes away on my fingers. Charon trails behind me a few steps, seeming just as wary as me.

In my city, wood was so foreign, so rare, that it could only be found in the richest family homes. It was something I never saw until I took over Allen Cloudspire's life. To see this level of destruction, and know that there's likely no way to grow them back, discomforts me. *What did they come to here?*

I stand and continue my slow progression towards the group of people.

"Charon, be prepared to take action if things get...violent."

He disappears behind me a few paces, fading into the darkness. As I march closer to the firelight, a small contingent comes out to meet me. There's four men, built like brawlers, and a child, a young girl around ten I think. They all wear white pants and jackets, and although covered in stains and tears the cloth looks thick and warm. The cut of their clothes, and the nearing fires, makes the chill more oppressive.

Dotty and I left our city in the same waterproof, technical fabrics we'd explored it in. The clothing is black as night and tightly sculpted to not impede movement. I'd appreciate it in a rainstorm or on a run. But it offers little insulation, and if I spent long in the cold air, I'd trade them happily for what they wear.

As the group nears me, plasma blades extend in the hands of two of the men. I still have my hidden blade tucked on my right wrist, my gift from Micah, but I'd probably be dead before I got close enough to use it. I stop where I am, and raise my hands in what I hope is the universal sign of being unthreatening.

The group closes the distance, and their features come into focus. The four men are covered in scars and have long beard growth. One is missing a hand, and another man is missing his arm past the elbow. Next to them, the young girl looks cherubically innocent. Her hair is long and golden, and her eyes sparkle keenly in the dim light. One of the men with a plasma blade steps forward. The flickering firelight illuminates a great scar that clefts his face across a void where his right eye used to be.

"What are you? Where do you come from? Helen tells us that she saw you exit the door at the top of the tower."

"I'm a man, same as you. Flesh and blood, no monster or machine. A traveler between worlds. I lived in a city much like yours, although it was in better condition when I left. I come in peace, only seeking to learn what happened here."

The man narrows his good eye, trying to read the truth in my face. In the corner of my eye, I see him idly turning the glowing blade in his hand. I wonder if Charon could intercept him before he cut me down.

"How'd you get through that door? And what do you mean, a traveler between worlds?"

I'm about to answer when the man missing his arm interrupts me. He looks less like a fighter than the others, or at least lacks the raised scars that cover their exposed skin. His clothing is cleaner and less torn.

"Damian, you know Edward wanted to question the man, let's not break our oath out of curiosity."

Damian sighs, but keeps his narrowed eye on me. He steps slightly to the side and gestures for me to go in front of him with his plasma blade. I follow behind the armless man, with the rest of the group trailing behind me. I take note when the slight buzzing sound of their plasma swords disappears. These blades have finite, although incredibly long-lasting, charges. These men are trained to preserve power and resources.

We make our way down into the encampment. The smell of burning overwhelms me as we draw near, and smoke from bonfires washes over us continuously. Though as we step into the firelight, I welcome the warmth they provide. Ragged men and women in all white stand around the fires and openly watch me as our group passes, hugging their children to themselves. When we get near the mass I saw in the distance, my heart sinks for these people.

The center of this camp is a giant mound of torn books, chopped wooden furniture, ripped paintings, and other priceless works. They're all fuel, likely looted from the surrounding buildings. I think of all the collective knowledge and art that's in that pile, and left for scraps. As I watch, a young boy dumps an armful of books on a pyre. It roars and spits upwards, and the boy settles in front of it, blind to whatever mysteries were on the pages. My heart aches for his future.

I'm led around the mass of kindling to the back of the camp. There's a large pavilion there, where Sun Gate families used to congregate for picnics in the brilliance of the park. The once open-air building stands double my height, and has been walled in with random debris taken from nearby houses. It looks like a pile of trash that someone carefully set a metal roof on top of.

We enter, and my eyes adjust from the flickering firelight outside to the interior. A stove sits in the corner, and firelight from it splits the room diagonally. The chimney from it spits upwards and out the side of the trash walls. The arc of light illuminates a table in the center of the room that's spread with ham, bread, and cheese. For the first time since I entered the Cosmos, I feel the sharp pangs of hunger.

A gray-bearded man sits behind the spread, slathering a piece of bread with butter using a massive metal knife. Despite his gray hair, there's nothing frail about him. The firelight casts shadows of the long scars that cross his muscular bare arms and neck. They have the peculiar puffy shape left by the cut and cauterization of a plasma blade. He sets down his knife, and stares up at me with dark, intelligent eyes.

"Ahhh, you must be the *traveler* then." He motions to the chair across from him.

I wonder how he knew the same word I used in my introduction, and the confusion must show on my face. He taps his ear, and I see the small com unit there. The men who led me here must be wearing them as well. *Armed escort, battle coms, is this a war zone?* I move forward and take the chair across from him.

I try not to stare at the spread of bread, cheese, and butter, but my growling stomach gives me away.

Laughing, the man hands me a plate. "Please, eat. We have plenty of food for our expedition." Looking over my shoulder to the escort he says, "No need to wait in here, stand outside." The men behind me shuffle out of the enclosure.

"Thank you, I hadn't realized how hungry I was." I grab portions of each food, and the man hands me his knife to cut off cheese and put butter on my bread. Showing I am no threat, I use the knife, and pass it back to him hilt first. He lets me take a bite of bread before starting his questioning.

"My name is Edward Meadowhearth, what's yours?"

"Nicholas Fiveboroughs." At this response, one of his eyebrows arcs upwards.

"I knew Nicholas. You are not him." *So their naming is the same here...and their city subdivisions. Is this another rule established by the creators, then?*

"There are more cities than this one, but they are all the same. Did you know this? I come from outside of this city."

The man's eyes narrow. "I heard this once, a long time ago, but I wanted to hear you say it. Tell me, how are you able to travel between cities?"

"Honestly, I don't have much more information about it than you do. I was given a key to the door at the top of that tower, and had to flee my own city before I was killed. I was chased by automatons, guardians of our city, do you have them here as well?"

The man nods slowly. "We did, before the city went dark and cut power to non-essential functions. Who was it that gave you this key, then?" From the look on his face, I think he knows my answer. The moment coalesces around me, and I realize this interaction may be much more interesting than I originally thought.

"An old man, he called himself the Narrator. From the look on your face though, I think you knew I'd say that."

Edward nods, and looks to his right, into the darkness. The ribbon of light from the stove frames him in profile, and illuminates the wrinkles that line his face underneath the beard. He's silent for some time, and then turning back to me, pulls out a necklace that was tucked into his shirt. On the end of it is a palm-sized metal coin that glints in the firelight. He pulls the worn leather strap over his head, and looking at the coin one more time, sets it in front of me. The unmistakable face of the Narrator stares back at me, etched into the surface of the gray metal. Even though the likeness isn't hyper detailed, I swear I can see a playful glint to his eyes.

I raise my head and stare into Edward's eyes, questioning. He sighs deeply. "It's a long story, but I imagine you want to hear it. I'll tell you ours, if you tell me how you came to meet the man."

TWO

DOROTHY

T he control room is sterile and clean. I saw the lights coming from the various instrument panels through the room, and when I stepped from the Cosmos through the door, soft lights turned on all around me. The room looks perfect, like it's never seen intrusion from anything living. I pace over to the window, and stare out into the black abyss. The light from the room makes my form reflect on the surface. I can't differentiate where I end, and where the empty expanse begins in the image.

A red light fades on and off on a control panel near the window. I walk slowly over to it, and on the screen above it there is a continuously repeating message.

Warning: Trajectory miscalculation. We have passed the intended destination by 4.8 light years.

I look around the stainless steel paneling that surrounds the screen, but there seems to be no interface for it. The technology looks familiar, but somehow archaic and advanced simultaneously. I ignore a sudden desire to solve the problem, to figure out how to work this machine. A lifetime of patient planning has taught me that prudence is the better part of action. I focus my attention on the room more broadly instead, and absorb what I find.

If this city is as old as ours, it's seen a very different life. Even our control room, though it was barely accessed, was dirtier and more cluttered with an assortment of things. I close my eyes and bring an image of the memory back to me, knowing that there's some major difference here. The layout of the room looks the same, although much of our instrument panel seemed turned off. Maybe it was damaged in the landing? An image floats in my mind of trailing my hand along our city's control panels, and my hand coming back with a thick layer of—

DUST! That's it!

My eyes snap open, and I run my hand along the mirrored metal in front of me. It's completely free of dust. I look in the corners, in the hard to reach places, and see no collection there. This hasn't been cleaned recently...there's just no dust being generated in this city. I look to the door that would take me into the large antechamber, and wonder what I'll find on the other side.

Dust is primarily dead skin, sloughed off in the natural course of living. It gathers and collects, a vital trace that life has happened. In Sun Gate of course, there was never dust that accumulated, but only because we had the technology to make it so. Cleaning robots rotated twice a day there, barely seen or heard, to give the illusion of perfect order. Cleanliness is next to godliness, and certainly the denizens wanted to believe themselves such. But even the robots would leave behind small traces, mistakes, imperfections that an attentive eye could catch. That's who I've always been, the girl interested in finding the cracks in their order, the things that reminded me it was not perfection.

I sigh at the memory, and let it go. Slowly, I walk over to the city's entrance to the control room, and it slides open to reveal a sparkling cleaning room. I remember going through our own room, covered in the ichor and filth from our battle with Cerberus. I see Nick, immediately ready to fight the cleaning robots, and then the calmness that spread over him on realizing they were not an enemy. There was so much he never knew about the city, so much I never told him. So much about me that he never knew. I smile at the memory of him, but when I remember the bitterness of our arguments afterwards, the smile fades.

Refocusing, I walk from the control room through the adjoining bulbous tunnel of the cleaning room toward the giant chamber that housed Cerberus in our world. The door opens, and I take a step back in surprise at what I find. My eyes dart all over the enormous room, taking it all in.

Pods long enough for an adult human are arranged in front of me. They're set into a column, and alternate to the left and then right of it to improve the packing density. It stretches from the floor to the ceiling. I look up, and remember our fight with Cerberus in our city, and how high that ceiling is. Next to the column is another, and another, forming a row down the entire length of the room, and next to this row is another that leaves only a narrow walking path between them. I'm amazed by the sheer scale of it. Rows of floor-to-ceiling pods fill the entire massive room.

Slowly, tentatively, I walk down the closest aisle, pods stretching above my head on either side. They're made of a smooth, reflective metal, and look seamless in construction. Inlaid on the top is an interface screen, set right beneath transparent glass. The glass calls to me as I walk by each one, pulling me to look into it, but respect makes me keep my distance.

Logically, I know what must be in these. I see them, and know our city must have started the same way. After landing at our destination, there must have been a great awakening, the birth of the only world I've ever known. This is how our story started, suspended in life pods as we sailed through the silent expanse of space. To see it here, frozen in infancy, still waiting to finish the journey they started so long ago...it feels sacred. I step quietly, as if afraid to wake them.

But it pulls at me, and I can't keep walking by the pods. My curiosity insatiable, I tiptoe next to one of the pods. The glass is thick so I have put my face nearly against it, and angle side to side to limit the distortion. Like a distant image that suddenly comes into focus, the dead walrus-like face of Edmond Sungate rises from the pod.

I scream and throw myself backwards, landing haphazardly on the pod behind me. Memories of the party at Skyball flood me. Everyone vomiting blood, death all around me, and all of it at my own hands. I've had weeks since then in the Cosmos, alone, but the visions of it still keep coming back. I look down at my hands, there's no blood on them now, but I can still see how they looked that night. *I did what I had to do. If I hadn't killed them, our city never would have changed. I brought justice.*

In a rush, I see images of everything it brought. I remember Brian tying himself to the Box to save Nick's life. Nick was raving the hour before that, telling us both how he loved us, and Brian didn't think twice about it. He was calm, methodical, but still afraid. Before I turned the machine on, our eyes met, and he only nodded at me mutely with panic in his eyes. At the memory, I clamp my eyes shut as tears well up. *Nick was right to hate me.*

I pull myself back together. *I did what had to be done, I'm not an evil person.* There was just no way to prevent the spillover of casualties, but it was all to forward necessary change. I stand again, and approach the pod I just looked into. I will not let fear of my memories dominate me. I walk back to it, and stare into the thick glass again. Staring back at me is a hollowed corpse face, but it's not Edmond.

I hear tapping. It starts quietly, but grows quickly. The metal on metal noise resonates through my memory, and panic wells in my chest. *Inquisitors.* I leap into the aisle to race back to the door, but find my way blocked by one of the automatons. Standing at the start of the aisle, its lanky, angular body and blank face fill the passage between the pods. I brace to fight, and reach down for the plasma blade that's still at my side, but the machine raises one of its pointed hands in a peaceful greeting.

"Peace daughter, I am not a danger." The voice is smooth, calming, and wholly different from the Inquisitors of my city. Their flat, inflectionless voices remind me only of the great violence they're capable of. There's a subtle softness to this one.

I straighten, and remove my hand from my blade, but do not respond.

"Are you a traveler, daughter? I have not seen one like you for many years."

"Yes, I'm a traveler. What are you?"

"Welcome then, traveler. I am this ship's Great Mother."

As we speak, the machine slowly moves closer until it stands only a few arm lengths from me. At this range, I don't know if I could reach my blade before it closed the distance. But I don't feel danger from it.

"Great...Mother?"

"Yes, daughter, these are all my wards." At this, the automaton sweeps its hand to signal the rows of pods. "I'm charged with their protection, and awakening when we reach our destination." The Great Mother pauses, and then in a voice of steel that raises the hairs on my neck, says, "Do you mean my wards harm?"

"I mean no harm, I am just a simple traveler," I respond quickly, and raise my hands in a sign of peace. This thing may sound less dangerous than our Inquisitors, but I'm certain it can be just as deadly if needed. Motioning to the control room behind it, I say, "I saw you were adrift from your destination."

"Yes, daughter. There was one like me charged with navigation, but they malfunctioned." I catch a hint of sadness in their voice, and wonder how long this machine has been alone. "Unfortunately, I am not equipped to understand navigation, or to change our course."

"And what of your wards, mother? Are they safe in stasis?" I think of the corpse face I saw in the pod, and wince.

I nearly hear the machine sigh in response, and it summons something uncomfortable inside me. *Is this thing, this Great Mother, experiencing emotion?* "No, daughter. The stasis pods ran out of life support many years ago." Its voice drips with guilt now, leaving me in shock. I watch the machine as it struggles to say the next words; "My programming prevents me from awakening them before we reach our destination."

At this, the machine actually hangs its head. How long has this thing been out here in the dark, watching its purpose die and being unable to do anything about it? Has it grown in the shadow of that grief?

My curiosity is piqued. "Great Mother, will you tell me your story?"

The machine seems to brighten, its shoulders raising slightly in excitement. "Yes, daughter. Come with me." It turns around, and walks back down the aisle, towards the control room. I follow cautiously, still watching the automaton closely for signs of danger.

At the end of the aisle, it turns left. We pass row after row of pods, each meticulously arranged in the same configuration. The silence of the room feels oppressive now. I look down a row of pods, their columns stretched floor to ceiling, and I shudder. I felt an air of possibility when I entered this room, but now I know it was just the breeze that blows through a tomb and reminds you of the living that exist outside it.

I follow the Great Mother to a room that's built into the wall at the head of the last row. It's a small metal structure, but tall enough that the polished metal doorway stretches above the automaton. On the side of the building is a pile of metal things. I realize as we grow closer that it was something once very similar to the Great Mother. But now it lays in a heap, like discarded trash. She doesn't draw attention to it, so neither do I, and when she walks through the main doorway, I follow behind.

Inside, lights set into the ceiling illuminate a private living space for two. It's austere, but not completely lacking the lived-in feeling of a place with a human presence. The room is full of precisely placed metal furniture—nothing is set askew or cluttered. Two charge stations are set into the far wall, and nearest the door is a small table with two curved chairs at opposite ends. The smell of aging paper hangs heavy in the cramped space. Lining every wall of the room, except for the charge stations, are shelves packed with books of all shapes. I look around at them in awe.

Turning back to me and looking sheepish at my fascination, the automaton says, "Over the years, I have started to enjoy reading. It does not take me long to read the words in a book, but it has taken me a long time to understand their hidden meanings. Now, I probably read slower than you, Daughter, but in some of these books I find such richness in a single sentence that I will think on it for hours."

I stare at it, dumbfounded. Never before did any Inquisitor give any sign of humanity, of sentience. Hearing it from her, it's astounding. "Where did you get them from? In my city, books are scarce and the wealthy hoard them."

"What a sad place that must be. This city never formed, so all the books we traveled with are still in the various floors of this same building. It was designed to be a nexus of civilization, the perfect place to start from. Every charge cycle, I travel to the other levels and pick out a new book, and return one of my old ones."

She looks at me and leans in closer, her posture open and hands slightly raised, and I realize her body language looks like excitement. It's strange to recognize it in a machine, especially without facial expression. "Since you are a traveler, are you hungry? We have a food synthesizer here, but I have never needed to use it."

At the mention of food, I realize that my stomach has been growling for some time. Since Nick and I entered the Cosmos, I haven't felt the need to eat. But now back in a city, it hits me like a wall.

"Yes. I think I'm starving actually, but I'd completely forgotten."

In a rush, the Great Mother turns and touches a panel near the charging stations. It slides open to reveal a keypad and a deep cavity behind it. She enters several strings into the keypad, and then my senses are overwhelmed by the smells that come from the synthesizer. One after another, the machine pulls out succulent green vegetables, baked potatoes, and an entire roasted chicken and sets them on the table in the room. I sit down in one of the chairs and stare at them.

In my city, no one in Sun Gate would use a food synthesizer this way. It was considered low class to pull cooked food from them. Instead, raw food was ordered and prepared by specialty chefs. No one in the lower levels knew about the food synthesizers, of course. There was so much technology in Sun Gate they didn't know about. Vendors in our district sold raw food to those that could afford it, and to those that couldn't they sold the nutrient blocks that the synthesizer used as raw material. The hoarding of food production always disturbed me, but right now I couldn't be happier to see one of the damn machines in full operation.

Lastly, the Great Mother gives me a glass of water and silver-ware, and sits down across the table.

"Please eat, daughter. I will tell you my story afterward."

I dig in, slowly at first but with growing voracity as I taste the food and realize my hunger. The automaton watches me, and even though her face is blank I could swear she beams in happiness.

THREE

DOROTHY

As I eat, the Great Mother starts her story.

"I was made in a factory, but it is hard to communicate how long ago this was. As the speed of our city has increased, our time scale has grown separate from our reference. In my years, it has been thousands, for Earth..." She shrugs at the thought.

"I became aware as we moved down the assembly line, just the same as all the other Great Mothers and Fathers. I remember being unable to move, as my central processing unit was still finishing connections to the rest of my body. And so I stared at the back of the head of another like me as we slowly moved down the line.

"We were one of the last things to be made, the final protection to carry their seeds across the universe. The Cities were already made, the people selected for stasis, and the destinations and flight paths charted. There was a finality to our creation that I saw in all of their faces. We were the door closing on their Earth."

As I listen to her, there is something like emotion in her voice. It's like a quiet brook next to a waterfall, but it's laced in every word. I realized then that I had stopped referring to her as an object in my mind, something no Inquisitor had ever convinced me of.

"They made us for this—" She gestures to the walls around her. "To watch over our wards and wake them when we reached our destination." After saying this, her head hangs for a moment, as if some moment of internal pain halts her speech.

"Our flight path was known as one of the longer journeys, but there were some longer. Each city was supplied with enough life support chemicals to make the journey, and enough spare to account for up to one year of drift. The scientists were always so sure in their calculations...

"I do not know why they only programmed me to take care of the pods and the wards inside of them, or why they only programmed the Great Father with navigation and ship maintenance. I have audited myself hundreds of times and I always see that there was space in my processor for both. They could have programmed us both with all the same knowledge.

"I asked the Narrator about it once—"

I hear my fork clatter against the table, and realize in hindsight that I must have dropped it. A cold, animal fear races through me. "Who did you just say?"

Her head tilts up a bit, appraising me I think. "Ahh, the Narrator. Have you met him as well? I did wonder, since you are a traveler like him."

What was the Narrator doing here, in this dead city, talking to an automaton? Nick said he watched every city, and had watched our struggle in our city. What's his aim? What sort of thing is he? How long has he existed?

"I have heard of him, but I haven't met him personally. Sorry, please continue." My mind reels with questions, but I turn my face stony. I want to try and gather some more information before I discuss it with the Great Mother.

"When I asked the Narrator about it, he said it had to do with the probability involved in making decisions. The scientists were concerned that one of us would reach a decision point that required a calculated gamble, and they didn't want two conflicting voices causing inaction. The more I read from their history though, I wonder if they just wanted to assign the same roles of *Mother and Father* they had enforced in their society." She shakes her head at this last bit, and the bitterness she feels is clear. This one decision likely robbed her of the ability to steer the ship to the intended destination.

"Does the Narrator come here frequently, then?" I ask, trying my best to keep the deep interest from my voice.

Her blank face pauses for a moment before answering. "He has come several times, but only after our route changed. Usually, he asks me a series of strange questions. He was the one to show me how to access the books downstairs, and encourage me to try and read them."

"Your route changed? Sorry for distracting from your story, please continue." There's something going on here, but I sense that my question was annoying to her so I hold back the follow-up that I really want to ask. *A series of strange questions? Like a Turing test?*

"When we were still a year's journey from our destination, the Great Father malfunctioned. It is important to understand that nearly all my functions are paused during charging. I do not need to do it frequently, I might last as long as a month without. The Great Father and I would alternate our charge cycles so that one of us was always aware, and so in extreme situations we might be able to wake the other from their charge sleep."

"My cycle was not disturbed. I completed it normally, but when I woke I could not find the Great Father in the pod bay. It was our practice to meet the other after a charge cycle to update them on progress. Understanding that something had changed, I went to the control room. The Great Father was there, crumpled into a heap on the floor, and a message played on the control panel that our trajectory was off course."

My blood runs cold at this. Is there an explanation for a machine, built to outlast civilizations and always steer true, to suddenly veer off course and then collapse? The scene echoes an outside actor.

She hangs her head again, clearly distraught at the memory. "I have inspected the Great Father deeply, I have disassembled him to learn what happened, but there are no clues beyond one minuscule burn mark. All of his central processing units seem to have experienced a great electrical surge at the same time. We are heavily shielded from magnetic interference, and certainly anything that affected him would have affected me, as well as the city. I cannot understand why he would have altered the course, either. He gave no inclinations of malfunctioning, and surely his last charge cycle would have assessed and fixed any issues."

Her blank gaze lifts to meet mine again. I can feel the pain there even if I can't see it.

"When we passed our destination, we were close enough that I could still see surface features on the planet. It was covered in large oceans of water. It was not just livable, it was an ideal planet—and we sailed right overhead. My programming prevented me from altering the course, or from waking up my wards early, so I could only watch as their salvation passed underneath us. And then keep watching as they slowly ran out of life support, and died."

I reach and grab her arm across the table before I even realize. It's a deeply human way of offering comfort, and by extending it towards her, I recognize her existence in a subconscious way that maybe no one ever has. I see the hallmarks of surprise in her slight flinch before she puts her other hand on top of mine, and lowers her head in acceptance.

"I'm so sorry, Great Mother."

She nods at this, but doesn't respond. I choose my next words carefully.

"In our city, the Narrator watched a great deal of suffering, despite being able to stop it. He told us that he enjoyed the drama of it. This is why I was interested to know that you had met him several times. Will you tell me more about your conversations with him?"

She nods several times, slowly. "I would always find him in this room after a charge cycle. The first time, I noticed immediately that he did not register on my scanners. There was no heat, or pulse emanating from him, but he did have physical form of some sort. He told me '*I do not really exist here, what you see is more like a shadow.*' He explained that he watched over all the cities, which were connected through the door in the control room.

"The Narrator wanted to understand if I possessed consciousness. I did not understand that at first, but after I began to read more, it became clear. This is why he would come immediately after my charge cycle, when all of my experiences are integrated into my core programming. Sometimes, he would ask me a series of questions similar to a classic Turing test. Other times, he would seek to understand my own perception of existence. He would ask if I wished I could cry, taste food, or smell. Sometimes we would look at artwork in the galleries below, and he would ask me what they made me feel."

I feel a pit in my stomach opening as I start to see the outlines of what might have happened here. The magnitude of it is horrific, insane.

"I confronted him once to see if that was his goal, and he laughed heartily."

He said, "'*Yes, that is my aim, Great Mother, but I fear I lack the appropriate tools to do so. Through the history of humanity, they tried to understand if an artificial intelligence was conscious through the lens of their own humanity. They would see how closely the subject replicated human consciousness. It was the only comparison they had, but no one truly understands what machine consciousness will look like, or if it is always the same. So I am like an artist trying to paint a picture I cannot see clearly with brushes and paints that I know are wrong. What I understand from this process is up to my interpretation.'"*

The *they* in that response catches me. *Is the Narrator not human? Or was he just referring to a previous time?*

"When I would ask the Narrator if he believed I was conscious, he would shrug and reciprocate the question."

I have to ask it, "Do you believe that you're conscious?"

She looks at me and shrugs. "If someone asked you that question, would it matter more what you thought or what they thought? *'I think, therefore I am'* holds very little weight without the validation of others." She pats my hand, still resting across the table on her arm. I realize that my answer was already given.

"If you're not conscious, then it's not a separation that I'm capable of judging. I have never met another machine like you."

She nods at this in quiet acceptance.

"Great Mother, will you show me the remains of the other like you? I believe I may know what happened here, but I want to check before I say anything."

She is surprised at this, but nods and stands from the table. Together, we leave the small, metal house, and she walks me towards the pile of machinery rested against the outside wall. I can make out the individual parts, but they've been nearly completely disassembled. Wiring and circuits sit with pieces of the smooth, metal exterior that is more familiar to me.

I sit down with the pile, and with great respect pick up each piece and inspect it. The Great Mother sits next to me, and watches my gaze as I sort through the remains. Each exterior plate is smooth and unblemished, lacking in the small mark that

I'm looking for. When I get to the torso drum I find it's too heavy for me to lift, so the Great Mother helps to pivot it around for inspection. On the back of it, I find what I was looking for.

I put my finger into the tiny dimple. There's still a small scorch mark present where the flare of electricity from a proximity EMP penetrated the resistant hull. It must have been a similar device to the one Nick used against the Inquisitors. I miss him sharply and deeply. As the knowledge of how cold and cruel this world is, and the games the Narrator plays come into sharper focus, I wish I had Nick's warmth beside me.

"What is this mark? Is this the sign that you were looking for?"

I look back at her with tears in my eyes, and nod. "This is the flare from a proximity EMP, it's a weapon that exists in our city as well. It's one of the only ways I've seen to destroy automatons. I believe that the Narrator used this device to destroy the Great Father, and then altered the course of your city."

"Why would he do that?"

I wish then that I could see her eyes to understand if there is confusion in them, or if it has already turned to rage. "To see if experiencing grief on the grandest scale–" I sweep my arms to gesture towards the life pods, "could be a catalyst to create sentience in you."

As the full realization comes, she drops the torso drum back onto the scrap pile. Her long, pointed arms go limp to her sides, and I can see her slump inwards. The weight of her consciousness bears down as it learns of its own genesis, the spark that let it grow. I understand the survivors' grief too well. Internally, she's weighing how incredible it is for an automaton to have truly stepped into awareness with how terrible the cost was. Hesitantly, I reach out and place a comforting hand on her shoulder. She ignores it, and slowly turns to walk back to her home.

"I need to charge, please help yourself to more food. You can find somewhere more comfortable to sleep in the libraries downstairs."

She lumbers slowly into the high-roofed dwelling, and the lights inside go dark. I hear the sounds of her starting to charge, and then silence drops over the room again. I look out over the pods, down to the pile of parts at my feet, and a shiver runs through me. Waves of nausea and anger course through me at the knowledge that an entire city was sacrificed just to try and create sentience. Nothing is worth a mausoleum on this scale. I wonder, did the Narrator think the ends justified the means here, or does morality not trouble him? Will I find justice anywhere in these cities, or just an endless stream of abuses?

I leave the rubbish of the Great Father, and walk the quiet aisles of life pods. Like before, I stay well away from their viewing ports, now certain that they only contain death.

The library is a different world altogether from the spare stainless steel and glass surfaces that greeted me in this city. The elevator doors opened one floor down to a world of obscenely tall bookshelves, wooden furniture, and plush, maroon carpets. I immediately feel the higher humidity in the room, likely controlled that way to preserve the books and wood. I walk past a kiosk meant to assist in selecting titles, to pace between the towering bookshelves. The place feels as quiet as the pod room above, but somehow brimming with more vibrancy and life. It's more of a sanctum of human thought than the crypt I was in before.

Ascending out of this room is a tall, wrought iron spiral staircase. It climbs to a door in the ceiling. In a flashback, I see Nick rushing up those stairs, his hands bloody from fighting the Inquisitors that chased him. He crashed through the door in the ceiling, and I waited on the other side. A spot in my heart aches at the memory. I wonder what strange worlds he's found.

I wander slowly between the stacks, letting myself get lost as I think. In our city, the Narrator watched suffering for generations so that the ground was fertile for revolution. He relished in the story it created. Maybe he even had an active role in nurturing it that was invisible to me and Nick. Here, he knowingly sacrificed an entire population to try and create sentience, all to sate his interest and enjoyment. We thought ours was a profound injustice, but now I wonder what vile acts we'll find in other cities.

I'm aware then that I've walked into the aisle of Greek mythology, and realize how fitting it is. Their gods treated humanity as playthings. The cruelty and callousness in their tales shows the bored hands of immortal toddlers that see the world as theirs to manipulate. The parallels are obvious, and anger flares in me at the thought of being a pawn for the enjoyment of the Narrator.

Past this aisle, I find a reading lounge with several plush chairs. Their soft, walnut-colored fabric calls to me. The weariness that's been building through the day hangs on my shoulders. Like some strange magnetism, I walk straight to the closest chair and sit down, reclining it until it resembles a bed. I sink into the soft cushions, and the heady smell of books, paper, and wood fills my nostrils. It carries me to the world of my childhood.

I'm young again, sitting with Sophia on the cushioned windowsill in our family library. We've just wrapped up my lesson for the day, which means it's my favorite time of the day. The two of us will lounge in the artificial sunlight, and she'll read to me from her favorite stories in our collection. It was always incredible to me that a family from Meadowhearth would be so well read. The heat builds in the windowsill as currents of paper and oiled wood blend, and waft over me. Together they wrap me in a wonderful cocoon, until I drift on the sound of Sophia's lyrical voice, and doze.

The motion-sensing lights that came on when I entered this floor turn off soon after, and my mind drifts in the dark, foreign space until I sleep.

FOUR

NICHOLAS

Edward and I finish eating, and move to sit near the fire in a pair of walnut-colored sitting chairs. In the flickering firelight, I can see they were stunning once. Now they're stained and have holes burned in the cushions from floating ash. The flames warm me more, completely cutting out the chilled air of the city, and with my stomach full I feel sleep tugging at the backs of my eyes. *When was it that I last slept?*

As we ate, I was concerned that Charon would think I was in danger. I should have known better. As I look over the old man's shoulder now, I see the great cat's eyes reflecting firelight in the darkness. He's my shadow, of course he found his way in. I consider calling him to me, but decide to let him stay in the shadows. Just in case.

Edward pours me a steaming cup of nutrient tea, I know the smell from across the room and smile at the memory. You can take the man out of the Boroughs, but you can't take the Boroughs out of the man.

He hands it to me, and from his expectant eyes I realize that it's a test. "In my city, we call this nutrient tea, and only those in the lower level drink it. Is that the same here?"

A smile plays at the corner of his mouth, a curving shadow in the firelight. "It is, but we just call it brine here. I wanted to see if you'd recognize it."

I take a sip of the warm, salty liquid. "Just as dense as my ma made it, thank you. I smelled you making it, and was reminiscing on how many nights I sat around a table with her drinking the stuff."

He nods in response, staring away from me still. He's silent, so I start on my story.

"In my city, we had a machine that could transfer diseases from one person to another, I think that's the same here?" He nods to me again, but now I have his attention. "In ours, those on the lower levels survived by taking on diseases from those that had resources to trade. We called them Sickos back home–"

Edward snorts. "Humanity is forever cruel I guess. Here we called them Pests."

"I was one of them, in a time that seems so long ago, and I wanted nothing more than to tear it all down." I continue, and Edward looks shocked. My golden hair and muscled frame are likely not what he considers typical for a *Pest*. "I nearly died from a metastasized cancer, and with the money I got from the job, I was able to change into the man you see now through facemelting—"

"What's that, then?" he asks, brows furrowed.

"DNA-assisted body modification. I don't know specifics, but it transformed me into a physical copy of a recently deceased Cloudspire. His memories were implanted afterwards, and merged with my own. We became something new together." Edward's eyes have grown incredibly wide, but he doesn't interject. *I guess facemelting is a curiosity of our city then.* "I won't go into the specifics of the journey after that, but I was able to use this new position to infiltrate the Medical Authority tower. When I accessed the machine that I thought controlled the disease transfer machine, it transported me to another plane where I met the Narrator.

"He told me a story of our past, how all of these cities were seeds of civilization flung into the stars, and how the disease transfer machine was created to control population numbers in the enclosed city. I was able to change things for our city, to open it up to the habitable world that surrounded it and change the disease transfer machine to cure all diseases, but I was pursued by automatons. I had broken into the tower, fought my way past them, and the city saw me as a threat. The Narrator gave me a key that allowed me to travel between worlds, so I fled." I'm careful to not mention Dotty or Charon, I don't need Edward knowing that there are more travelers just yet.

He's stunned, and keeps staring at me for a while. Then he blinks several times, and shakes his head. "That's quite a story, traveler. What a curious thing it must be, to see cities that look like your own but have a different history. There must be endless wonder out there."

"This is the first city I've found that isn't a crypt. From what I can tell so far, many cities haven't survived, and some are deadly even to enter. The most *wonder* I have found is in the heat of this fire and the food you gave me."

He nods at this, absentminded or unconvinced. "Your story starts so much like ours, I wonder how many other worlds suffer the tyranny of Capitalist masters."

I arch my eyebrows upwards at this, but don't prod with a question. I've said nothing of the economic and political realities of our city, I'd never even thought about it much. *Was this a truer cause of our oppression, or would it have happened regardless?*

"I'll start our story on a street corner, but of course there are centuries that lead to that moment. The lower classes, the Pests chiefly among them, were tired of being kept under the heel of society. A rage simmered in the streets that all could feel, and with every starving child and early death it rose and rose until violence was inevitable.

"It started as an increase in thefts, fights in the streets, and escalated from there. Our streets became so dangerous that no honest person would walk them after dark, no matter where they came from. It was so bad that those grisly automatons would patrol them, but they were few and our rage was endless. It flowed in the streets where they were not.

"We did not know the impotence of fighting each other, until he showed us. With no more than a voice amplifier and a chair to stand on, he preached from the street corners of Meadow Hearth. Not of gods and religion, but of politics. He decried the horrors of unfettered Capitalism, he showed us how we were cogs in a great machine."

We had similar street corner preachers in my city, but no one paid them any attention. They shouted about everything, usually incoherent, drunk, or insane. A backdrop that formed the din of the streets.

"As the days passed, a crowd grew around him. He would teach us many things in that time, of alternate forms of government, of different thought through history, and word spread through the districts of a truth-sayer. For those who listened, we learned that our rage was misdirected. We had been hurting our brothers and sisters in our anger, and in doing so, hurting ourselves. Our fight was not with them though, it was with the society. It was with the shackles they made us wear.

"I was an early believer, and soon I spent every day listening to him. His words swept the streets like wildfire. The violence stopped, the anger paused, and we all listened. Besides his talking, there was silence. We became his children, his students.

"Meadow Hearth became unproductive. En masse, we stopped working, stopped contributing. We stopped offering our blood to keep their machine running. People helped their brothers and sisters instead. We shared our food with the hungry, and healed the sick amongst us. For the first time, many of us felt a beauty and rightness in our days, a glow that came from working together. In those short days, love flowed and our hearts were so full.

"We should have known, of course, that it couldn't last. A cog that doesn't turn can stop even the biggest machine, and nothing was more important to the society than the humming of that machine. Two Inquisitors came, and accused our shepherd of inciting a riot. The irony of it still haunts me. They walked through a street full of people sitting and quietly listening to an old man talk. And they called it a riot!

"When they tried to take him away, that was when we stood as one for the first time. We linked arms with our brothers and sisters, and said no. The metal devils tried to force their way through the crowd, to get to the old man, and that anger that had been held in check, that had simmered at a near boil for so long, exploded. But no longer was our anger misdirected, we knew the truth of it all, and our violence was righteous.

"The automatons never made it past the first row of people. Plasma swords appeared on all sides, and cut them down. We knew at that point the streets were no longer safe, more automatons would come and destroy us all. The preacher quieted our fears, and led us through the maze of tunnels underneath the city to hide. Occasionally, the robots would find us, but by then we were entrenched and prepared for them.

"On that day, we became one people with one goal—to tear down the machine that used us. We took off the yoke of the oppressors then, and became our shepherd's knights. We showed our devotion by crafting these pendants."

At this, Edward lifts the metal coin he wears around his neck and shows it to me again. The horror that was building in me through the course of his story becomes real, and crashes over me. A chill races up my spine, as adrenaline courses through me. The sleep and comfort I felt only moments ago is far gone.

"Wait, this man, this street corner preacher, was the Narrator?" I ask incredulously. He's there in my memory, laughing in delight at watching me struggle to change my city. I see him passively saying that he watches all of our worlds suffer. *Was he passive, though? Or was he creating the suffering, to see what we'd do?*

Edward nods in response. "That's correct, although I didn't know who he was then. When asked his name, he would always respond that he had none. *'I am the voice of your anger, I do not exist beyond that',* he would say. At some point during this time, he began to predict the future.

"I know now that he was not a seer, but at the time we all believed, or we did when it started to come true. He told us that darkness would slowly creep into the city as the machine slowed down, and we had to be poised to strike when it did. And so, we militarized. In secret, we gathered gear. We learned tactics of war. We trained everyone amongst us, the women, the children, the elderly. We knew this would be our only stand, our only chance, and everyone committed to it. And as we did, just as he said, the city began to shut down.

"It started with a slow cooling of the air. As if a fire was dying, the temperature ticked down day by day. At first, it was imperceptible, and then it was all we could think about. Did you ever realize that the city is kept at nearly the same temperature, constantly? I'd never thought about it before. We learned to shiver for the first time. The upper echelons of the city were in an uproar, no one understood what was happening.

"Soon after, their flying cars stopped charging. Sun Gate and Cloud Spire were set in a sudden paralysis, some of their towers weren't even designed with stairs. Overnight, residents were stranded in their ivory towers. The automatons that had sought us out were rerouted on rescue missions, and down there in the sewers, we laughed and laughed at their foolishness. It's clear now that we were just as foolish as they were.

"The darkness came last, with a slow dimming day by day. Our anticipation grew with it; we were hungry for the darkness, we had made a home with it long ago. The city was in chaos at this point, emergency councils ran constantly in Sun Gate trying to solve the problems, and trying to understand their source. Slowly, it became clear that the automatons were no longer able to charge either. We found them frozen in the street, stopped for eternity mid-task. As the lights faded, I noticed the same from our prophet. He secluded himself from us, the society he'd built.

"When the lights collapsed with a sudden snap, the dam that had been built around our rage broke."

He pauses here, and stares into the fire. It's clear now what haunts him. I can tell by the small number of people in the clearing, by the lack of other lights as I stared out across the city on the steps of the Medical Authority. I assumed at first that there were others somewhere else in the city, but if there are, it's no great mass. A chill goes down my spine as I realize that Edward is not a war hero, not a revolutionary—*he's a mass murderer*.

He continues. "A fever took us, it was like nothing anyone had experienced. I see visions now from those days of violence, and wonder if they're real. We ate through the city like a plague. There was nothing to stop us. All the technology that once protected these lofty heights meant nothing when the power got shut down. When the violence finally stopped, when our lust was sated, we noticed that our prophet had disappeared.

"To some, this was a sign that our righteous rage was satisfied. They truly saw him as a manifestation of our anger. I felt confused though, lost in his absence, and I didn't believe in the mysticism of it.

"Years later, I found the gate at the top of that tower. I stepped into it, and met the Narrator, the face behind the mask of the prophet. He told me he oversaw countless cities like ours, on countless different worlds. Seeing him there, I had never believed in him more. Until I asked him why he chose to guide our world, to free us from our oppression. He laughed in response, and said; *I helped you out of boredom, and to see what interesting place your city goes from here.*'

"In my stunned silence, he continued to tell me that our city existed on a planet that didn't see its celestial sun for an entire century, and that it then stayed in the sunlight for another five centuries after. He told me that our city is powered from that sunlight, and so now in our dark age we will live in this cold, dead place until it shines on our city again. He wanted to see if our small society would persevere, or collapse back to earlier ways of civilization, or disappear entirely. I realized then that he was not some benevolent god, not a wise prophet, but a child playing with dolls. We are his playthings, and to him, our lives are no more consequential than that."

Edward spits into the fire, disgusted. And I see him for what he is—cast out, used up, played for a fool. A husk of a man that is left only with his memories and his regrets. He bargained his humanity in the hope of creating a better world, only to realize that their messiah didn't guide them towards salvation, but its opposite. And now, he's stuck in this world that's slowly dying, and wondering how long their survival will last. How long until his people starve? How long until they collapse into violence over scarce resources?

It hits me now that I am not sitting at the fire with a friend, with someone who comes from a background like mine that I can understand. This comfort and understanding I've felt from our similar history, it blinded me. He knows what I am, knows that I can leave this place. I am here with someone trapped in a cage of their own design, and I have mistakenly told them that I have a key to leaving.

My mind blazes through possibilities as Edward and I sit next to the flickering fire. I feel for my wings, but they're like a numb limb. There's not nearly enough power in this city to charge them. Underneath my clothes, I'm still wearing the cosmic armor that saved me when we stormed the Medical Authority tower in our city. But my head is unprotected, and the armor will only slow the plasma swords of the four guards to this makeshift shelter. They all have combat training, I might die in minutes trying to fight my way from here. But I have a cat, and they're not expecting that.

I sling myself from my chair and bolt for the door, but Edward is impossibly fast. He intercepts me from behind before I've made half the distance. He wraps an arm braided with muscle around my throat to choke me. At the noise, the four guards at the door come in. They stare at me struggling in his arms. I lock eyes with Charon's yellow slits in the dark, and motion toward them with my hand.

"Sorry brother, but we need your key to leave this place," Edward says in my ear, and slams the knife from the table into my side. He had it this entire time and I didn't even notice, but he also didn't notice the impossibly thin armor under my clothes. He doesn't know what it's capable of. He is expecting the knife to pierce my side, tear into my vital organs, but instead all of the energy redirects backwards. All the force he puts into the blow travels back through the knife and his hand, and I hear them both shatter in an instant with a sickening crunch.

The next moments are like a flash of frozen images. Everything happens all at once, but I process each moment and respond. Edward screams, and his grip on my throat loosens. The guards at the door start towards us in momentary confusion until a shadow breaks free from the wall, and rips into them. I slip underneath Edward's loosened arm, pivot around, and spring the hidden plasma knife on my wrist through the bottom of his chin. His screaming stops in an instant with the hot smell of cauterized flesh.

I turn back around, and find the guards in a mess. They stand facing all different directions, confused and trying to find Charon in the dark. There are already several dripping gashes on all of them. The nearest of them is turned away from me, his plasma sword humming. I run to him and shove my knife through the back of his head. It sticks out through his forehead like a new, glowing horn, and he drops to the ground. I don't stop to fight the others. Instead, I rush through their confusion and out the door. I turn back to see Charon right on my heels.

Shouts go up through the shanty town, and plasma swords turn on all around me as people rush to join the fray. I embrace my conditioning, and the food in my belly, and sprint for the Medical Authority tower. By the time I make the stairs, I turn and see the gap to my pursuers is already growing. Behind them, I hear wails traveling up from the fires as people discover their leader's death. I slow my pace only slightly as I enter the tower and climb the long stairwell.

The run up the stairs is grueling, but I know however it pains me, it is demolishing the people behind me. I hear their panting breaths and flagging footfalls echoing all around me in a cacophony of sound as we ascend. My own breathing is ragged when we hit the top stop, and Charon next to me makes similar sounds. But we know where our exit is, and we race to it. Through the grand hall, and the cleaning room beyond, we reach the control room and the door that leads into the only home we have now. I throw it open, and we plunge through into the safety of the Cosmos. The door shuts behind us, and closes out the evils of another world.

FIVE

DOROTHY

I dream of my mother, a dream I've had so many times that I know its rise and fall like a well-worn book. She died when I was five, and my memory of her face and form are that of a child. She's haphazard, proportions all wrong for my now adult size. Her arms stretch down from above me, impossibly long, and lift me up to her loving face. It's a face that I can never quite make out in the dream, only her gigantic hazel eyes and curled black hair are clear. She holds me aloft and we spin in the sunlight, and I ache for a world where I grew up with this woman. With her beauty, purity, happiness.

A cloud shields the sun, and the dream changes. As it always does. There is no life where this dream ends in happiness. My mother's face draws in on itself, sharpening features, until she has to set me down. She's too tired now, too shrunken and desiccated. The cancer races through her, eating her insides, and

I feel all the anger and confusion of my youth rise back up. Why does my mother stay sick, when everyone else gets cured?

And then I stand above her, my hand coming down to hold hers. The sky darkens, and I smell rain at the window. She smiles at me, at the smell that she always loved, and closes her eyes.

I open my eyes into bright light, and think momentarily that the dream is repeating. This cruel loop of memory spinning around and around until I sink into grief again. Long arms reach down to me, and grasp my shoulders. A blank metallic face fills my vision, reflecting my own image of hazel eyes and dark brown hair. She notices my waking, and with a self-conscious-ness she retreats.

"Hello daughter, you were moaning in your sleep so I came to ensure you were okay," the Great Mother says, sheepishly. I am in awe again at how much emotion she expresses.

I raise the reclining chair I was sleeping in, and throw my legs over the side. I hold my head in my hands for a moment, rubbing my eyes to clear the weight of sleep and memory. *How long has it been since I had someone that cared for me? That would compassionately wake me from a bad dream?* I remember how I left her then, with the weight of understanding that her sentience came at the price of her grief. I want nothing more than to give her a way out from this tomb. It's an empathy I don't feel often.

"Great Mother, does anything hold you here still?"

She pauses for a long time, and looks around the room. This beautiful library that has been her companion and teacher for so many years. "I feel like I have been waiting for something since we passed our destination. Waiting to see if fate would guide us somewhere new, waiting to see if my wards would survive, waiting to see what came next. There is nothing left for me here now." Her voice is hard, angry.

"Come with me, then. I don't know how we find him, but we can't let worlds continue to be playthings for the Narrator. I'm certain his actions aren't just limited to your city and mine." My memories of grief were like a chrysalis, coalescing the cool weight of purpose in me through the night. A righteous rage builds in me now with every word. "He has to be stopped."

"You would have me as a traveling companion? I doubt that I will be useful."

I stand and reach up to put my arm on her shoulder. Her tensed shoulders ease under the weight of my hand. I consider covering up what I'm feeling, but something about her drives me to honesty. Maybe it's the loneliness from the Cosmos affecting me.

"I'm not looking for a useful companion, I'm looking for a friend."

As we move past the life pods again, I notice the contemplation in her steps. She walks slowly and looks to either side of her, as if saying goodbye to her wards. I follow behind her silently, giving her the time she needs to come to peace with leaving this place. When we get to her hut, I follow her inside.

"Great Mother, how will you charge once we leave the city?" I say, realizing the oversight.

She shrugs at this. "How will you eat? It is just as likely that we find a charging bay for me as food for you."

She walks the shelves of books, her hands tracing their spines. She pulls them down, and opens to a random page as if sampling their taste. Most of them go back to the shelf, but a rare few she spends longer with, and then tucks them carefully into a compartment that opens in her chest.

There's a doubling as my memory overlaps with the scene, a pervasive sense of déjà vu. I watch her and see Sophia, my old caretaker, her hands caressing the backs of books in our family library. I see the love for them in the care she takes, the reverence she has as she holds them.

"Great Mother, the others of you that were made, were they called the same thing?"

Clearly distracted, she nods. "I was not an individual from them."

I walk up behind her and thread my arm through hers from behind. It feels silly, but it's been so long since I had a friend, and I've missed this. "But you are an individual now, and anything sentient deserves a name. Can I call you Sophia? You remind me of someone I used to know."

She pauses, and then sets her hand over mine and gives it a light squeeze. Even with the blankness of her face I can tell how touched she is. "Thank you," she whispers and nods.

Sophia packs around a dozen books into her chest cavity. When she turns around they are neatly lined up like she's a walking bookshelf, and I can't help but smile. "You will have to read them to me," I say and Sophia nods again, as a silent door slides out and shuts the books in securely.

I follow her out of her home, and she walks directly to the Great Father's corpse and kneels. There are no words, she simply spreads her hand on his torso piece and leaves it there for several moments. When she stands again, she stares out past me towards the rows of life pods. There's closure in her bearing, like she's taking one last image of this life before leaving it forever.

She nods towards it, and then approaches me. "I believe I am ready, how do we travel?"

"Follow me," I say, and we walk across the Great Hall and through the cleaning room. I'm wondering if it will spray us down again, but apparently whatever I've picked up here isn't as offensive as when I stepped through with a monster's guts drying on me. We walk through unmolested and into the control room.

When we enter, Sophia walks over to the repeating computer message, and shakes her head. Then we walk to the window that shows nothing but an endless abyss and stare out silently for some time.

"Do we travel through this?" she asks me, and I shake my head and point to the antique door in the corner.

"Through that...it's some sort of different dimension that allows us to move quickly between cities. But I have no sense of direction there, no clue which door to head towards. Maybe you can make more sense of it than I can. But first, I need to try and visit our mutual acquaintance," I say, and point to the dimensional transit device.

It looks just like the one I forced Nick into back in our city, and a pang of guilt stabs me as I walk past Sophia towards it. I swing open the door, and nestle my body inside the cavity. For a moment, I imagine how Nick felt as the door shut, so sure that it was the last thing he'd see.

The world around me fades, and is replaced by darkness. I'm surrounded by an endless expanse of nothing, but like a slowly forming dream, a light flickers in the distance. I walk towards it, but it feels like I'm floating. No sensation returns to me, no air brushes against my skin, and if it weren't for being able to see my own body I'd think I was just a consciousness floating in this void.

I expect the Narrator to show up suddenly, and keep glancing around to find him. If he is here, he seems disinterested in me. As I get closer to the flickering lights, I see that they're dimly illuminating sitting room furniture. I move forward and find two armchairs with an ornate wooden table in between, completely devoid of any personal artifacts. Both of the chairs look equally worn, as if someone was careful to not have a favorite. Awash in the flickering light now, I turn to find it coming from a bank of screens that yawns above me and stretches several feet in either direction. Every single screen plays the same series of images, over and over again.

I'm rooted in absolute horror as I realize that I'm watching a video of the attack on the Skyball, then it switches to show me shoving a needle full of tranquilizer into Nick and Charon, then to me forcing Nick to sacrifice himself to turn off the disease transfer machine. And then it repeats, endlessly. A knot of anger and shame burns in my gut, building and building, until I roar like an enraged beast, run to the screens, and try to put my fist through one. My arm passes through without stopping. In the light of the screen it's semi-transparent.

I scream in frustration, pulling my arm back and turning from the wall of screens. Turning from my shame, my regrets. Those things, I performed them like they were a duty, something that had to be done to achieve my goal. They seem so evil when shown like this, devoid of the end goal. Separated from the justice I was trying to bring to the city.

"I'm not your fucking villain! You're the one playing god in these worlds. You ruined an entire city here. I'm going to find you, and I'm going to destroy you!" I scream into the void, shaking in rage. I know that he's out there somewhere, watching me. And as I peer into that darkness, searching for his eyes, it fades. With a snap, I'm back in the city, sitting inside an anthropomorphic cavity with a transparent covering, and Sophia watching me on the other side curiously.

When Sophia asks what I saw on the other side, I tell her only that the Narrator didn't show up, but left something there to mock me. She must see the rage still cooling in my eyes, and doesn't push further.

We walk over to the door, and I grab the handle. Up until that moment, I hadn't wondered if it would open for me. Nick was the one given the key of course, but I just assumed that it would apply to me as well. For a moment, I consider the possibility of being stuck in this dead city forever. Living out my days reading books with Sophia doesn't seem like the worst possible outcome, but still I feel relief when the knob turns in my hand and the door swings open.

Sophia gasps as the Cosmos is laid bare in front of us. It's a sound I've never heard from a robot before, and it makes me smile. I grab her cool, metallic hand and we step through the door. The endless sea of Cosmos is stretched beneath our feet, with row after row of doors peppering the horizon.

Sophia is stunned, and looks around repeatedly to take it all in. "This is magnificent. I believe this is a fourth-dimensional plane. Time has stopped here, or at least my internal body clocks have. The creators must have built this as a means of transit between cities, any other means would be infeasible since they would be at such extreme distances. These doors must contain wormholes, then. I see a path stretching in front of us, do you just follow that?"

I stare at her, dumbfounded. There are so many questions I have now, but all I can think to utter is, "Path?"

"Yes, this semi-transparent tunnel that stretches into the distance. I believe it is some sort of probability density function made physical, likely it protects us from being three-dimensional beings in a four-dimensional space. Or maybe it just protects us from getting lost. Can you not see it?"

I grab her arm. "Sophia, I don't understand. There's a path for us to follow?"

She chuckles at this. "Yes, and likely you followed one here, to my city, as well. Since it contains the weight of the probable future, it would be extremely unlikely that you could deviate from it."

"So then, our path is set? Our destination is already determined? But who set it?"

She shrugs at this, and taps the place in her chest where the books sit behind. "'Men are mistaken in thinking themselves free; their opinion is made up of consciousness of their own actions, and ignorance of the causes by which they are determined.'"

"What's that from?"

"An old philosopher, Baruch Spinoza. In truth, I think we cannot know the answer yet. There are some thinkers who believed it was always this way, predetermined. This may be just a more visual example, or it may be that this is a requirement for dimensional travel that we do not understand."

"But which way does the path head?"

"I would guess that if you took a random step it would be the same direction."

As if to prove a point, I take a big step at an obscure angle to my right, and then another at a different angle to my left. I look back at her, and she nods to confirm I'm on the path. I get down and crawl several paces forward, and then jump up like a frog. I look back and find Sophia chuckling, and nodding. She walks from the door to join me as I sit down, dumbfounded.

She crouches and sets a hand on my shoulder. "Had I not told you, it would be the same. The weight of knowing does not seem to change the outcome. Maybe it was set when we entered this space, or maybe it has always been set."

I nod at this, and wonder how she can see this path and I can't. *Something hidden in her programming? Maybe she was intended to be a guide between cities?* Then I stand, and I'm about to ask her what direction to head when I realize it's needless. The words freeze on my lips. I strike out randomly, a different direction than I approached this door from, and she follows beside me.

We pass doors as we tread the field of Cosmos, but I don't go to them. It's not that I'm waiting for the right door, or waiting for some feeling, but the knowledge that my path is already set in a direction keeps playing in my head. I wonder then, if I hadn't invited Sophia to travel with me, would my path have been different when I entered the Cosmos? Or do the paths travel our world as well, invisibly pushing us to a destined future? What feels like hours pass, and we keep walking forward. The scenery changes slowly under our feet, and I realize it must represent the real locations of these cities. If only that was meaningful to me.

Eventually, I see a door on the horizon that directly intersects the direction we're walking. There's this inevitable gravity to it, like it's drawing us in as quickly as we're moving towards it. We cross over solar systems, traverse galaxies, and then stop in front of the door. I can't help it and turn towards Sophia, looking for some approval still that I've gone in the right direction, and her blank face stares back at me and nods once.

I put my hand on the door knob, and open it. On the other side is a majesty I have never experienced.

SIX

NICHOLAS

I wander the sea of stars, Charon at my side. We pass doors into other galaxies, and at every one I pause. Behind that, is there another civilization on the brink, another one that's in the middle of eating their own tail? The fight we had in the last city keeps replaying in my head, showing me scenes that I'd rather forget. My plasma knife protruding from Edward's head. I can still feel the pressure of his body against mine as he went slack, smell the roast of his flesh. *I killed him with such...callousness.* For what might be the fiftieth time since we left, I stare down at my hands and wonder what great and terrible things they're capable of.

After we made it back through the door to the Cosmos I rested on the other side. I slept, and dreamed that I had left the door open, and the hateful abuses from that world crept over the Cosmos and infected all the other cities while I slumbered. In my dream, I woke to find that all the remaining cities were demolished by genocide, civil wars, tyrants. And with each new city I discovered thereafter, my depression deepened. We had birthed our civilization into the stars, only to find that we sent our hate, greed, and power lust.

I finally wake and find a similar feeling reflected in Charon's eyes. I scratch under his chin and around his ears until his great purrs rumble against me. It brightens us both. Rising, we strike out on our path across the stars.

A child playing with dolls. The phrase Edward said keeps replaying through my head. *The Narrator is orchestrating these travesties for his amusement. Our cities are just his playthings.* A familiar anger burns through me as the faces of the people I loved, and lost, flash through my memory. At the centuries we've all spent in oppression, and the hand that guided us to it.

It's clear to me then. Fixing my city, turning off the disease transfer machine and opening it—it isn't enough. We are all still in the grip of the Narrator, and the only way we can ever be free is if he's gone. *He is the chain that binds us all, the Box was just a symptom. He must be destroyed.*

I walk past another door, and behind it in the distance, I see something new. It breaks me from my thoughts. I squint at it, unsure if it's really there, or just a trick of the eye. It looks like there's another path converging with my own, far in the distance.

The closer I get, the more clear it becomes. Another path is stretching out from my left, and joining my own in the distance. Excitement floods me as I realize that it must be Dotty's path. I'm running towards it and smiling, thinking that I'll see her behind the next door, or running down her own path.

Then I finally see the full picture, and my mood sours. I slow down, and can feel Charon's questioning gaze on me. The two paths merge at a doorway.

"I see Dotty's path, boy, can you see it?"

"*Yes.*"

"I thought she'd be on it, but I realize now that we don't know if that path is her future, or her past. We don't know if she's coming or going from that door," I say, and sigh deeply. She's the only one I can make sense of this place with, and I realize then how deeply I miss her. Even with her betrayal, even with her monstrous actions, I'd leap with joy to see her again. To hold her again.

Still, I know now that my future holds that possibility. If she could see the paths, she'd know it too. As I near the door, it becomes clear that her path is no longer alone, something very tall is traveling with her. I stare at the semi-transparent tunnel, trying to piece together what it could be. It must be close to ten feet tall, and in the shape of the tunnel its arms extend much lower than they should.

My stomach drops out and the hairs stand on the back of my neck as I recognize the shape. *An Inquisitor. Fuck, what has Dotty gotten herself into?* I imagine their pointed fingers tearing into her, and wince. She's obviously alive by her tunnel, but it's hard to imagine how well she's doing if she's traveling with one of them.

I'm left with a choice. I don't know if this is her past or future. I don't know if she's already entered this door. And to complicate things, she may be in danger. I can either wait for her here, or try to find her in the city on the other side. *If the path here was set, was it already decided what choice I would make? Is the weight of possibility real, or imagined?*

I should at least understand the shape of things on the other side of the door, if she has crossed through already I may be able to save her. I should scour the city for signs of her. I reach down, and open the door. On the other side is the familiar control room, but here it's bathed in beautiful, white moonlight that comes in from the viewing window. Nothing moves on the other side, so I cross over with Charon at my heels.

The air is muggy and wet, thick with humidity like after a rain in our city. I step carefully, keeping my movements quiet, over to the viewing window, and stare out in awe. A dense forest stretches out from the city, thick foliage from massive trees blankets the horizon. Moonlight washes everything in shades of white and black, making it look ancient and sleeping. I look down, comparing them against the city structure itself. They must be a hundred feet tall. As I'm looking downwards, I see that this city is open.

The petal-like landing bridges have extended over the landscape surrounding the city. It must have happened some time ago, because tall saplings are already re-growing at the edges of them. I look up into the night sky for the source of the light, but can't see the moon through this window. As my vision settles again on the horizon, I catch a gleaming white building on the far hillside. It seems to reflect the moon's glow, like a beacon. I set the direction in my memory, and turn from the window.

My eyes settle on the dimensional transit machine, the human-shaped cavity we used to commune with the Narrator in our city. It calls to me, and when I step towards it, it opens smoothly. I hesitate. I need to search this city for Dotty, but I also need more information about the Narrator, about what I'm up against. I weigh the outcomes. For the second time, I place my body in the opening, and the world around me disappears into darkness.

A board of alternating color squares coalesces in front of me. Across the board, various circular tiles are placed in the squares. A foreign hand, sun spotted and wrinkled, moves one red piece over a black piece. I follow the hand up, my vision floating higher in this sensationless world, to find the Narrator sitting across from me. He smiles a perfect smile with straight white teeth, a sign of youth juxtaposed with his age. I'd shudder here if I could.

"Seems you've lost another one, Nicholas. You'll have to be more careful in the future. Once the pieces are all gone, you lose." He says, holding the circular tile between two fingers. As I watch, his hand closes and reopens rhythmically, a tic that I hadn't noticed before.

"Is this a game, then?" I circle my finger in the air, indicating the whole space.

"A game, a story, they're all metaphors for life, boyo."

"In that, you insist on treating our lives like that's all they are?"

"In that, you're constrained by the walls and rules they create. Don't you see that? You follow your fixed path, your actions are constrained between moving to the left, or moving to the right." As he says this, one of the pieces on the board hops diagonally to the left over another piece, and then across one again to the right. They dissolve from the board, and appear in his hand next to the first.

"You're playing both sides." I say, but it comes out like a growl. Anger seethes through me.

"Of course I am! What other way is there to build drama and tension? Sporting matches are always best when the audience believes they're even, that any outcome is possible. Should I instead let you be trampled, defeated, embarrassed?"

"How do we win this game, then?"

"Win? You want to win? Hah! What happens then? Another game, another match? What *is* winning, my boy?"

I'm tired of his riddles, his manipulation. I'm tired of the reminder that I'm a pawn for him. I reach down and slap the board from the table. There's a flash of searing pain in my palm where the key is etched, but I ignore it. The game scatters into the darkness, and disappears. I gaze hatefully into the eyes of the Narrator.

"Fuck your games!"

"Ah! Nicholas, an inspired choice! You've chosen beyond the binary. You've found the hidden path to level the playing field. And now we stand as equals, laid bare without a game to shield us, to guide us. Remember this next time you're given a choice between two options, there are always hidden alternatives."

As he speaks, the darkness builds around me, and the Narrator disappears into it. By the end, he's only a voice in the void. The dimensional transport cover comes back into view, and I push it open. Only when my hand leaves a bloody smear on the lid do I realize that the key cut into my palm is bleeding.

Quietly, I make my way out of the control room, and through a dormant cleaning room. On the other side is the grand hall. The smell of the room hits my nose like a wall. Citrus fruits, mint, and basil at the edges overwhelm me as I see that the room is full of plants and awash in moonlight. The plants are growing in towering columns, reaching towards each other and crowding the thin aisles between them. I'm wondering how light is coming into this space, until I look upwards.

The domed ceiling has been drawn backwards, leaving this portion of the city open to the environment. I can see the moons clearly now, two of them hang nearly directly overhead, offset from each other. One is closer and larger, more white in its glow, and the other hangs further back, reticently giving off a yellowed light.

The differences from the last city I saw, from my own city, are remarkable. I'm overcome for a moment as I stare upwards at the alien sky, aware suddenly of how small I am compared to the greatness of all these cities, of all these worlds and the Cosmos between them. I shake myself from the reverie, and get back to the task at hand.

I saw no signs of Dotty on entering, but she could have been taken deeper into the city, or even to that distant gleaming building. There are no signs of life in the room beyond the plants, so I squeeze into one of the aisles to the door I know is on the other side. Long tendrils and branches slap at me, and the smell in such close proximity is intoxicating. This aisle appears to be mostly made from fruit, some of which I recognize, and

I stop to harvest a handful of blackberries from a thin shoot halfway across the room.

The taste of them is magnificent, and I close my eyes briefly to savor it. Their flavor is complex, with notes of mint and cinnamon, and I would stop to eat more if I didn't feel Charon's tail flick against my leg. He wants to keep moving, and he's right. I continue down the aisle, amazed by the grapefruit and oranges I see, and then become interested in some fruit foreign to me at the end of the walkway. It has a spiny husk that seems to peel near the top and is shaped like a bulbous teardrop. I move in to smell it, and there's an unfamiliar musky sweetness to it.

"We call it the slave's tear."

I whip around at the voice to find a tall, lithe woman in loose, thick overalls standing in the doorway and carrying a small pair of shears. Her skin is dark in the moonlight, and her short hair falls in dense curls. Even with the shadows cast across her features, it's easy to see she's beautiful. She raises her hands to me.

"I'm no threat, just a gardener. You a friend of The People?"

I struggle with how to respond for a moment. "I'm a traveler. I come from a city very similar to this one, but very far away."

"I don't know anything about other cities. How'd you travel here, then? You got a flyer?"

She speaks like we did down in the boroughs. Short, clipped sentences that say more with less. Listening to her, my history pulls at me. Since I took over Allen's life in the clouds of our city, I've lost this way of speaking. I'm a foreigner to myself.

I'm about to answer when she sees Charon striding out from behind me, and she jumps backwards, brandishing her sheers like a knife.

"The hell is that thing!?" she yells at me.

I hold up a hand to her, and slowly kneel down and scratch Charon's neck and fur. He sits obediently and arches into my scratches.

"He won't hurt anyone that doesn't mean harm, please put down those shears."

She lowers the shears slowly, but continues to stare at me dumbfounded with her body pressed against the door.

"We're alien to your world, but we come from a city that is just like yours. I was given a way to travel between cities. There are thousands like this." I think of all the desiccated wreckages I saw floating through space—*maybe not just like this.* "I am a traveler."

She musters her courage again, and pushes herself off of the wall. "You come from where that woman and her machine came from then?"

I stand again in a flash. "What woman? What did she look like? When did they come through?"

"Slow down now. They were just through here two cycles back. No one here wants to deal with machines, too many stories we heard about them. We all hid and watched them." She smiles ironically. "Couldn't see much, but anyone could tell she was real pretty. Is that your boo, then?"

I flush, and she laughs at me. She seems free and unguarded in that moment, without a trace of self-consciousness. "Alright mister, you don't seem like a bad one. Follow me and I'll show you around."

She sets her gardening shears down inside, and we exit out the door. I felt it when we entered, but this city's core is still functioning. My wings twitch on my back as I follow her down the hall to the elevator.

"So that woman, did she seem okay? Was she safe?"

"Seemed so, she was jabbering on with that machine of hers. Most folk here stay inside during the day time anyways, too hot otherwise, else they would have seen us."

"The machine, it wasn't forcing her?"

She laughs at that. "They were practically walking arm in arm. I'd say they were thick friends, if that was possible."

What the hell has Dotty gotten herself into? I think as we approach the elevator door. It slides open noiselessly. The interior is bright and clean, but decorated with small tables of plants. I reach out and hold one frond in my hand. The flat green leaf nearly covers my palm and feels soft to the touch.

"So, you like the plants? These here are my doing, same with the greenhouse. I'm Jasmine, by the by." At this, she puts her hands together, palms flat, and bows slightly. It's a gesture I've never seen before.

I imitate her gesture, hoping that I'm not being offensive. "My name's Nicholas. You built that greenhouse? It's magnificent, I've never seen anything like it. In my city, barely anything grows."

"What do you eat then?"

"Mostly these small blocks of nutrient rich—"

"Wait, you eat that shit? Nasty! Yeah our city's got 'em too, but we haven't had to touch em in generations."

I laugh at this. Then I remember that Edward's city was separated into the same districts as mine. "Is your city split into districts? I come from Five Boroughs, down at the bottom."

She stares at me for some time before answering. "I haven't heard it called that in a long time, and only then in stories. When The People took the city over, they got rid of anything that divided us. Now there's just The People, and the city. We all live where we like."

I'm about to ask more, but the elevator door opens, and I follow Jasmine out the steps of the Medical Authority building. We exit the building, and my understanding of this whole place shifts. Moonlight streams in and blankets everything in a soft glow. It makes the city look ancient, but far from dead. The park in front of me is a thick mass of towering fruit trees, organized garden beds, small ponds, crop fields, and serene paths that me-ander lazily through them. The moonlight dances over it all in serenity. People fly amongst it all on wings like mine, collecting food in baskets and watering crops, silent in their movement in the dark.

I sit down on the steps, floored by the sight, and realize only then that I'm crying freely. *This is what the city always could have been. It's how we always should have been.*

"You okay, mister? You never seen people fly before?"

I wipe my eyes, and stand back up. "Sorry, it's just, what you all have built here is beautiful."

"Just some fields and trees and such, you don't have that in yours?"

I see a vision of Edward's city, where they burn irreplaceable knowledge and art just to stay warm. I see this same park, with every tree cut down and dead. "You have no idea just how lucky you are, Jasmine."

She nods at this seriously, absorbing the weight of it, and then continues walking. "Well, when The People moved back here, they wanted a way to make this place right for their families. So they planted, and now we tend the fields. You want me to fly us down to the city, mister? I can probably carry you."

I smile at Jasmine, and let my wings spread for the first time since leaving our city. It feels like stretching my legs after they've been stuck in one position for too long. I flex them to their limits, finding relief in the motion, and then pull them back in. Jasmine smiles knowingly at the sight.

"Damn it feels good to stretch those! Thanks for the reminder, but I'd rather walk if it's all the same to you. Your city is magnificent, and I don't want to miss anything gliding above it."

"Have it your way then, follow me."

In the moonlight, people fly through the fields and garden beds as we walk on a path through the park. Things aren't planted in neat rows, but with some innate sense of beauty and naturalism instead. It forces the path to twist around like it's savoring some sense of wonder in the journey. I'm staring up into the treetops, and almost miss when someone is walking the other direction until Jasmine speaks. When she does, I look down to see a young boy frozen in fear and holding a half full basket of fruit. He's wearing similar overalls to hers, but his seem a size too big for his small body.

"Well stop gaping, Ash, or you're going to catch bugs in that mouth of yours. We got another *traveler*, just like that woman. I'm taking him to the edge of the city."

We keep walking towards Ash, who doesn't move or respond. When he sees Charon, he drops his fruit basket and runs into the trees. Jasmine chuckles and bends to snatch two pears from his basket. She hands me one, and dusts her own against her overalls before taking a bite.

I follow her lead. It's so sweet and pristine that I have to stop walking and close my eyes for a moment, overwhelmed.

"So your people, did they live somewhere before settling in the city?"

"Yes, they were slaves."

"Slaves?! To who?"

"You saw that big white eyesore up on the hill? A man lives there that doesn't age, he controls the whole damn planet." She spits. "The city here protects us, sends out machines if his men are dumb enough to try anything."

A man who doesn't age. Is it the Narrator? "Have you seen this man before, do you know what he looks like?"

"I've never seen him, just heard the stories." She turns back to me and anger burns in her eyes. "He still has them, you know? Slaves that is. They work the mines and serve him in the palace. We get a few that escape sometimes, but most of them get snatched before they make it here."

As we talk, we've continued through the city. She's taken me out of the place I know as Sun Gate. The entrance is overrun with vines and looks majestic. I've seen a few other people, but they hurry out of our way long before we reach them. We walk the path now down to the city exit. Lights burn in dwellings across the city, there are pockets of life everywhere here. We've passed several disease transfer stations, most are dark as a tomb, but inside one I see an old woman hooked into a Box alone. I stop and watch her.

"In your city, does that thing cure diseases?"

"Yeah, I heard it used to work differently before the city opened, but no one remembers why it changed."

Someone met with the Narrator, that's why. I tear my eyes off the woman using the Box, and we start walking again.

"So the slaves, why not try to free them?"

"Oh people have tried through the years, failed mostly, or they come back with a handful of new folk but lose more of our own while they're at it. The guards have melters and ships that fly, we just have pointy sticks to wave at them from the ground. It isn't a contest." She spits again in anger.

We've been walking down a street that grows brighter with moonlight with each step. At the turn of a corner, we're suddenly at the edge of the city, and I'm staring down one of the unfurled sides into the forest beyond. The trees tower upwards, as tall as those towers of Sky's Reach that impressed me so much in the past. Their canopy is lit in a majestic, soft glow, but everything underneath is dark. A lazy wind blows through the trees, and that same musky smell from the unfamiliar fruit washes over us.

"Not safe out there, if you haven't guessed that already. Patrols everywhere, traps in the forest, all to catch runaways and bring them back. That white castle you saw—" She points down the ramp, "is straight ahead, maybe five miles. As long as you're walking uphill, you're going the right way. That woman of yours, that's the direction she headed. No saying if she made it to the palace now, but that's probably your best bet."

Her eyes dart left and right, avoiding mine, and she chews on her bottom lip in concentration. Something is making her nervous. Is it being so close to the boundary of the city?

"I got to tell you one more thing, only I'm not sure how because it doesn't make any sense. Before she left, that woman got into some sort of fight."

I bristle, wondering again about the robot companion. "What happened? Please, tell me everything you know, even if it sounds strange."

"Now I wasn't there, so I didn't see this with my own eyes. And stories being what they are, well you know, it's likely to be a bit inflated."

"Was she okay afterwards? Was it the robot?"

"No she was fine, and it wasn't the robot. I heard she was talking to a real old man, and things got heated. Well next thing she drew her sword and tried to chop that old man in half, and the robot tried to pummel him too I guess. But...it all just went right through him, like he wasn't really there, and then he disappeared afterwards. Now likely this is just people telling tales—"

"It's not a tale, I think I know who that was." My fists are clenched so hard pain flares across my knuckles. "After this happened, is that when she left the city?"

"Yeah, sorry I don't have more to tell you. From what I heard, she left right after."

I close my eyes and breathe in deep, consciously relaxing the tension in my hands and arms. When I open my eyes, Jasmine stares at me. "Thank you for telling me what you know, Jasmine. I'm sure this will help me find my friends. And thank you for showing me your city. I've seen a lot of things, but nothing quite so beautiful as this place."

She nods at this and bows again with her palms flat to each other. I respond in the same gesture, and start down the ramp. From up in the control tower, its size wasn't apparent, but from here it looks nearly half a mile long. The forest starts abruptly at the end. It's a curious thing, walking on these panels that used to make up the walls and sky of a city just like mine. I find my mind drifting back to my own then, and think of how my people must have felt walking down these walls. I wonder what my mother thought at the sudden freedom, and there's an ache in my chest. *I wish I had been there to see it. To see them all drinking in that first sunlight, to see them all get what they deserved.*

My mind is drifting, so it's no surprise that I don't see them sooner. A small, flying craft, flat and only long enough for the two men standing on top of it, zooms above my head. It's close enough that the rushing current of air it brings with it blows across my body. I whip around to follow it, and see it leaned over in a hard corner to race back towards me. Wrap-around visors on each of the pilot's helmets are fixated on me, coolly reflecting the moonlight.

Only then do I hear Jasmine screaming "Run!" from the opening to the city, but I don't need the encouragement. Charon and I are off already, racing down the ramp and to the woods. At least there, I might be able to hide. I'm fast, but

Charon's like a shadow racing through the night. He quickly outpaces me. I see the flying craft coming in from my peripheral, and put my arms above my head to shield it.

And then I'm flying, tripping over my own feet and soaring through the air, propelled by my momentum and a sudden slackness of my muscles. A curious pressure rocks across my body, making me woozy and nauseous. I sail towards the end of the ramp, and right before I hit the ground, I catch sight of Charon running off into the woods.

I collide with the hard metal, and pain pinballs through me as I ragdoll across the end of the ramp, and into the surrounding dirt. When I finally stop moving, I try to stand, and find my equilibrium is gone. I keep getting up on my hands and knees, and falling back over. The nausea is overwhelming, and I puke in the dirt underneath me, and fall right back into it. *What the fuck did they do to me?*

I'm trying to crawl towards the edge of the woods when the flyer lands behind me. The heavy boots of the two pilots crunch through the hard dirt behind me.

"Now, now, you're feisty! Hit ya with the sonic cannon, does hell on your inner ear. Likely you're feeling pretty terrible right about now."

"Look at the rat, he puked all over himself! Shoulda known better than to leave your hole, rat!"

A swift kick from one of the armored boots goes right into the side of my head, and sends the world spinning down into a sudden darkness.

SEVEN

DOROTHY

Sunlight streams in through the window, highlighting motes of dust that float lazily in the control room. In a flash, a memory of those days of my youth surfaces, when I'd lay in a warm windowsill and listen to Sophia read stories. The fake sunlight of our city would arc across the carpeted floor, and the dust would dance through it.

"Interesting, there are other paths connecting to this door," Sophia says behind me, peering around us and into the Cosmos.

"Other paths? Wait, what do they look like?"

"One is taller than yours, broader, but definitely still human, and the other is low to the ground, maybe some sort of animal?"

"Nick and Charon, they're here!"

I rush through the door, thrilled at the possibility that I'll be reunited with the two of them. The heat and humidity on the other side hits me like a wall. It blankets my skin, cocoons against me as I run into the control room to the viewing window. Colossal, hundred-foot-tall trees stretch out in every direction, their canopies colored in a kaleidoscope of reds, oranges, yellows, and purples. The beauty of it catches me off guard, and I forget racing after Nick as I stare out at it.

Sophia walks up beside me, and appraises the view in silence for a time. "Unfortunately, we do not know if your friends are here, yet."

"What do you mean?"

"I believe that the paths show where they will go, but not when they will go. We may be chasing after them, or running from them."

I nod at the wisdom, struggling to mix it with a brewing curiosity to explore this new planet. I analyze the desire coldly, wondering at its root. I'm pulled to this place, but for no discernible reason. *Is the Narrator pulling us here?* As I'm thinking, my eyes wander the landscape, and I see a giant, gleaming white palace in the distance. I fixate on it.

"I think we should at least explore this city. If Nick is in front of us, we may find him. If he is behind us, I'm certain he'll make the same decision."

I turn from the viewing window, and walk out of the control room. Sophia follows me, and when the door to the great hall opens in front of us, we stop at a wall of plants on the other side. The layout is so reminiscent of the life pods in her city, but wholesome and living instead of sterile and dead, that the two images overlap in my brain. It brings some peace to that memory. There's a welling happiness in me at the sight of so many thriving plants. It's like the gardens from our city, but chaotic. This place is truly alive. The walkways between towering columns of plants are choked with vines and leaves, filled with that haphazard growth of real things. A soft breeze blows in, sweeping down through it, and all the leaves move lazily. It almost looks like a greeting, and I smile at the thought. It takes me a moment to realize the ceiling is pulled back, exposing real sunlight to the room. *This city is open, then.*

A trickle of sweat races down the small of my back, and only then do I realize how oppressive the sunlight is. The heat and humidity seem to magnify each other, and I'm reminded of a terrarium my father kept in his office. Over the years the plants inside grew to their container, until they completely filled the space, choked themselves off from the light, and died. The glass of that container was always covered with dew from the internal humidity.

I walk towards the aisle of fruit with Sophia trailing behind me. The smell of rich, ripe fruits of all kinds mixed with soil and moss fill my nostrils as soon as I walk down the aisle. It's heavenly, and I stop to pick several fruits on my way. Rare tastes of blackberry and strawberry swirl on my tongue, they're magnificently complex. I'm not greedy, and just sample a few of each as we go through. Behind me, Sophia grabs the vines and shoots, examining them.

At the other end of the room, the door is opened slightly. Sophia and I leave the rows of plants behind and move into the shade. The coolness chills my skin, and I realize how much I was sweating under the sun's gaze. We move to the elevator at the end of the hallway, and I'm touched to find potted plants decorating it. I push the button to take us to the ground level, and wonder what we'll find on the other side of the door.

When I see the planted crops, organically sculpted orchard, and small ponds that fill the landscape of the Sun Gate park, I let out a strangled cry and sit down on the steps of the Medical Authority building. Sunlight filters in from the open sides of the city, illuminating everything and casting long shadows. The wholesomeness is so disparate from our own city, where only the very richest would ever see this park, and anything wild about it was manicured out of existence. Sophia sits next to me, as in awe as I am. We don't speak for a long time.

"I believe we are being watched. There is movement at the windows," she says quietly, so as not to draw attention.

Without turning my head, I glance around at the buildings that surround the park. There's a flutter of curtains in one of the windows, and I know Sophia is right.

"Do you think we're in danger?"

"I think we should keep moving, and pay attention."

I feel the weight of eyes following us as we navigate the city. Sometimes, from the corner of my eye, I'll catch a sudden movement, a fleeting retreat, and know that we're still not alone. It feels disturbing, being watched like this in a foreign place. But we continue on our march through the city, navigating down from Sun Gate to the basin of Meadow Hearth, where we can step outward into the surrounding forest.

Plants grow everywhere—in entryways to buildings, windowsills, and down the length of the sidewalks. It's not just functional plants that provide food either. Thick-leaved succulents decorate the walk in greens and purples. I don't feel in danger, despite being watched. Being surrounded by all these plants shows a nurturing touch to the city. Instead, I find myself reaching out to draw a hand across the plants, as if I can share in that love they were made with. It's a version of the city that feels wholesome and right.

When we pass the building that in our city was the Metal Oyster, I'm reminded of Nick. The night we spent there gave me a hint of who he really was. It was when I actually started to fall for him. Not the pretend attraction that I feigned earlier, when I only knew he was some imposter that I could use, but a real connection. The care he showed for others, especially those he didn't know, was so foreign from my life in Sun Gate. In this city, the building has the same shape, but it seems to be some form of communal living space. Hand painted signs are propped against the exterior announcing *Rooms Available,* but no price is given.

We turn a corner, and both Sophia and I stop. From here, the city opens into the landscape beyond, and the view is magnificent. The trees that we saw earlier from the top of the city soar above us now, their colored leaves visible only when I crane my neck upwards. A heady scent of hot tree sap and wood winds into the city on a lazy breeze. It smells foreign and seductive. We walk closer to the exit from the city, but are stopped again when an old man seems to materialize as he walks up the ramp from the outside.

Sophia recognizes him first, and reminds me of the cold threat of violence her body carries. Her books and blossoming personality can distract from it, but just like the Inquisitors of my city, she can be a weapon. She extends her sharp, pointed fingers, joining them into a lance, and bends her legs as if ready to lunge at the man. I'm surprised at her reaction, and then study the figure that walks towards us closer. His wizened face and tuxedo are incongruous with the city, something from a very different time and place. Then I recognize the face from the brief moment I met him in the Skyball, and in the same instant reach for the plasma sword at my hip. *The Narrator.*

Still several paces off, he stops and spreads his hands wide, and gives a slight bow. The smile on his face seems to mock our anger. My hand grips the plasma blade at my side. I long to show him how well I know how to use it.

"What a scene you set! My two favorite ladies, off on a new adventure together, exploring foreign worlds in search of their missing friends. They wander into an unknown jungle, certainly full of danger, in the setting sun. Will they find them? Or are their paths destined to continue like two parallel lines, never again to cross?" He pauses and looks around. "The natural lighting here really is fantastic, have you noticed? I couldn't ask for better—"

"Here to despoil another world? Or have you already had your fun with this one, and now you're bored?" I say. Both Sophia and I are like coiled springs, ready to attack, but he's standing too far away. *I wonder if I can lure him closer.*

Something I said gives him pause, and he idly wanders forward while speaking. "Oh my dear, I don't do this out of boredom! Well, maybe it started that way. I help humanity to achieve its full narrative potential. I am but one small cog to help guide it on the path. I'm only here to tell tales, sow intrigue, spread rumors, and yes, I guess to nudge the plot in a direction befitting the actors. Without me, imagine how poor and chaotic your stories would be."

"You manipulate our worlds for your own enjoyment. Our lives are not some damn playthings," I say through a clenched jaw. My body is one singular, taut muscle, ready to explode. *Only a few paces off now, can I cover that distance?*

"You are a monster, and the stories you create are not legends, but horrors," Sophia says, rage sharpens her metallic voice.

"Ladies, ladies, please." A few steps closer again, he's almost in my blade's strike zone. "Wouldn't it interest you to know how to find your friends?"

My body is tensed and ready to spring, but his offer seems to gum everything up. I can feel the conflict in the alternating waves of intense hatred for him and the deep concern for Nick and Charon. *Are they okay?*

Sophia is the first to speak, "Tell us what you have to say, devil."

The Narrator turns his eyes on me, and they bore into mine. They are deep black, like the Cosmos reflects in them, or are made from the same substance. There's playful intelligence behind those eyes, and it seems at odds with his appearance. His face is wizened, with deep set lines of age crossing it, and his shoulders stooped from fighting gravity for too long.

"Your friends are trapped by
A gleaming white mystery
That never grows old,
A practice common
From birth to the stars beyond
Of men over men,
Feed this hungry world
A freedom so long foreign

To find them again"

His message delivered, he bows deeply, and both Sophia and I spring at the same moment. She is lightning fast, but the distance is small and her inertia is greater than mine. I reach the Narrator as he's coming back from his bow. My plasma blade moves as an extension of my hand, my foot sliding forward in a slashing lunge that I've practiced since I was little. The blade ripples to life, slashing blue death across the Narrator as it parts him from hip to shoulder.

But something is strange, the blade should part flesh easily, but offer some resistance. There is none, and the expectation of it throws my weight off balance. To counter the momentum from the swing, I have to carry through by planting my outside hand and cartwheeling gracefully over it. I land ready to strike again, but find the Narrator whole and unaffected.

I watch as Sophia makes contact with him, or tries to. Her leap carries her into him, her sharpened metal fingers held together like a spear point. It plunges into the Narrator and should rip a hole into him, but she keeps traveling *through him*, and barely catches herself on the other side.

Standing now, the Narrator winks at me, and then laughs as he dissolves into thin air.

The forest foliage is so thick, the sharpness of the day faded as soon as we entered the trees outside the city. A hundred feet above us, the leaves rustle in the breeze, and call down to us their message of idyllic repose. Shifting patterns of sun break through them so that on the ground, the light is constantly moving, fading, and disappearing, only to break out suddenly in a new location nearby. It gives the forest a transient, whimsical feel that is completely at odds with what we've found so far.

We saw the first snare hidden in the trees while we were still in sight of the ramp from the city. I nearly stepped on it before Sophia grabbed my arm. It was a simple pit covered by well concealed branches, and when I moved the branches to the side I saw a sensor lined cage sitting at the bottom. I stared at it for a long time, but it's intended cargo was clear. It's meant to catch humans. I've had a knot in my stomach since.

As we carve deeper into the dense foliage, we find more human snares of different designs hidden in the trees. Thankfully, Sophia is a master at spotting them, and guides us around the danger. But at each, I stop to study the design. They are basic and brutish, ankle grabs, trapdoors, cages to fall on the unwitting, but nothing that would maim or harm. They seem intentionally built to not hurt their prey.

We make our way through the forest slowly, with Sophia at the front. The ground slopes upwards constantly, a relentless hill climb. I've quickly lost any sense of direction in the thick foliage, but something in Sophia directs us towards the white palace. She is able to analyze images she sees and plot a course between them.

"Why would this world lay out traps like this? Do you think the people in the city are dangerous, and these are meant to protect those outside?" Sophia asks.

I think back on the stunning plants we saw in the city, the degree of care was evident there. It seems totally at odds with the city residents being hostile. "I wonder if it could be the other way around, actually."

"Do you think we should have trusted the advice of the Narrator? He may be guiding us towards his own intentions."

I hear his words again, and shake my head to clear the rising anger. "He is definitely steering us, but I can't tell how. We know we can't trust him, but we have nothing else to go on to find Nick and Charon, other than what he said. What do you think?"

"I think the logic of it is sensible, but I feel this path may be dangerous and not as we predict."

I nod in agreement. There's something coming, but we won't know what it is until it's too late. The comforting weight of the plasma blade hangs at my hip. There's a pleasantness in action, even if we're moving toward danger. The goal of finding Nick and Charon has given me a vigor that was missing in exploring the Cosmos. I'm staring up at the shifting light breaking through the canopy when Sophia's head snaps to the side and she stops moving.

"What is it?" I ask.

"I just heard faint laughter," she says, her blank face scanning off to our right.

"The Narrator again?" I reach toward the blade at my hip.

"No, it sounds like a female."

Sophia starts to walk towards the sound, and I follow in her footsteps. Both of us are alert, searching.

Another tinkle of laughter goes through the forest like the soft chiming of a bell. It's fanciful, carefree. Sophia crouches down, and past her I see that the forest is thinning. I crouch behind her, and we move slowly forward. I can catch faint conversations now, and the soft clinking of plates and glasses. I know these sounds viscerally, they stir memories inside me of nights spent in the embrace of society in our city. Nights of glamor and brilliance, nights that could let you forget the abuses that propped them up, if you let them.

As we move closer, the trees thin and we can see a small clearing of beautiful wildflowers. They blossom in pastels of indigo and cerulean, a surreal scene in the now fading light of the day. A picnic is set amidst them, and a group of twenty beautiful people mingle and lounge on blankets eating hors d'oeuvres. They are dressed impeccably in tuxedos and evening gowns, and with every step they trample the flowers in the glade.

Sophia and I watch them from behind the last of the trees at the edge of the forest, and stay silent to not draw attention. It's like watching a scene transplanted from the grand balls of my childhood. Conversations form in small groups, brilliant laughter floats upwards from politely guarded mouths, men show bravado, and women feign interest. Couples lounge on blankets at the outskirts, popping succulent treats into each other's perfect mouths, and austere waiters pepper the landscape in between.

Their luxury is plain, and I realize how far from that I've been. I look down at the torn athletic wear I've had since escaping our city. The cosmic armor Nick gave me shows from underneath the gaps in the clothing. I look at my hands, covered in dirt from the forest, and I remember I haven't bathed since leaving. I haven't thought about how I smell that whole time, but now I imagine if Sophia wasn't a robot, she'd be offended by it. Thankfully, it seems it was only sentience she developed.

I'm not afraid of these people, I refuse to be. I stand up and walk into the glen with my head high and back straight. Like a slow moving tide, conversation dies at my approach. Behind me, I hear Sophia's movement and know it's not only my appearance that's drawing attention. One by one, the revelers turn to stare at us. I look from one to the next in the silence. There's something strange about them, but it takes me a moment to see it. They all look around the same age, even the waiters.

"She is the traveler," a pretty man with a well-trimmed mustache says.

"She is the traveler," others of them say in agreement. There's nodding amongst the group.

Did they knew I was coming? Did the Narrator come to them, too?

A lithe woman in a revealing black dress steps forward to me. Her dirty blonde hair falls in loose curls over slender shoulders, and spills across her open neckline. Like the rest of them, she is beautiful. Her ice blue eyes fix on me, and when I look down from their gaze I notice that she wears no shoes in the grass. She stops several paces away.

"My dear, we waited a long time for you to come. There's someone who will be very interested to meet you. Come with us to meet the king." It's not a question, so much as a soft command.

A king? It takes a moment, but I find my voice again. "He lives in the white palace on the hilltop?"

The woman nods, and extends her hand to me. I turn and look at Sophia, searching her blank face for the wisdom I know is underneath the surface. The whole scene is reflected like a warped mirage across her face. She nods imperceptibly. I turn back, and reach to take the woman's hand in mine. Numbly, I follow her back to the group. As we near, the people part, and I have the strangest feeling that they are wanting to reach out and touch me, but restraining themselves.

Behind them is a large, flat craft with a small, enclosed pilot's room at the front. It's all sharp angles and gold trim, with a panoramic viewing window in the front. An ornate, golden railing curves around the edges of the craft. The woman holding my hand steers me toward it, and like we guide a flock, the others fall in behind.

EIGHT

NICHOLAS

I'm in the Skyball again, swirling in a room of masked faces. There's a fat man in a walrus mask that I'm trying to avoid. I keep seeing him in front of me, turning the other way, and then finding him in that direction. There's something coming, but I can't remember what it is. I see an end to the crowd of animal masks, and push through to freedom. On the other side I find the Narrator as I first saw him—an old man blending into a room of vultures. He smiles at me, a look full of devilish wickedness, and behind me the room disappears.

I want to ask him what he's done with Dotty, why he's playing god in all these different worlds, why his existence is an endless cycle of cruelty, but I'm mute. I'm trying to yell, to scream, but nothing comes out, and instead he speaks.

"The pain has all mixed with the pleasure until I can't tell them apart anymore...I just want to experience something new, but I think there's nothing new left for me."

And it dawns on me then, the point of it all. I hear what he was trying to tell me, and in this moment of realization the towering glass wall above him explodes into thousands of shards. I watch them dance in the light, a crystalline reflection of so many stars, as a tram rockets into the room.

"I just want to experience something new," he says again, as an endless stream of knives splashes over us, burying us, crushing us, killing us.

I spring awake in the same moment, dripping wet with sweat and with my head throbbing. There's a splitting ache pulsing from my right temple, and when I reach up to touch it a hand flies from the dark to slap mine away.

"Don't touch it, that needs healing. They smacked you proper."

I search the darkness for the source of the voice, and make out the edges of a man's face in front of me.

"Where am I?" I ask, my voice a harsh rasp.

I feel its dryness like a sudden new imperative, and as if the man knows, he extends a small wooden bowl full of water. I sit up slowly, making my temples throb even harder, and then grab the bowl and drink the cool water down. The tension in my head recedes to a dull roar as I lean against the wall behind me. The crumbling texture of dirt and stone rubs against my back.

"You a runaway, then? Patrol dropped you off this morning," the man says.

As I think of Jasmine, my recent memories come flooding back. Of the city of plants, of trying to find Dotty, of the patrol descending on me and sending me into oblivion.

"I'm not from here, I come from a different city, very far away," I say slowly, and then hesitate. "I remember being taken by a patrol as I left the nearby city—where did they bring me?"

The man's eyes bore into me in the darkness. "Well ain't that something. I figure you were from another mine, but I ain't heard of another city. Bad news though, this is a slave camp. And once you're here, you're one of us. Let me be the first to welcome you to south mine. We're good folk here. Work's hard, but we get three squares and the guards don't treat us bad."

I don't panic at the thought of being trapped here as a slave, not yet. It's too far removed from everything that came before. It doesn't seem real. As my eyes have adjusted to the faint light, I see that the man I'm talking to has long, dark hair tied into a loose ponytail. His arms are swollen with muscle, and round shoulders bulge from underneath a durable-looking workwear shirt. He doesn't show any signs of malnutrition. His skin is deeply tanned and streaked with dirt. I can't imagine he's any older than 25.

"What can I call you?" I ask him.

He pauses for a long moment, and looks upward as if searching for an answer. "Brian Meadowhearth was my city name, back before the mines. Mind you, don't use that much here. Most just call me Doc because I care for the injured. What about you?"

I stare at him in the darkness, memories swirling of my friend Brian and a wild hope springing up in my chest. I see the countless times I woke up to his face as he put me back together after another disease wrecked my body. I see his final sacrifice that let me keep living. I know that names are repeated in these cities, I know that this man in front of me has no relation to the Brian I knew, but still I search his face for similarity in the dim light. He cares for people here too, and I take some comfort in knowing that there are at least others like my friend.

"In my city I was called Nicholas Fiveboroughs, was there someone else here called that?"

Brian nods contemplatively before answering. "Aye, there was, something of a hero to us. He died trying to free us from the mines years back."

Is that a similarity to me? Are there traits that are the same in each city? I notice a new heaviness growing behind my eyelids, and a slowing of my thoughts. I look at Brian, and he sees the question forming on my lips.

"Wasn't just water I gave you now, you need sleep. There's a weed that grows around these parts, helps a man rest," he says, but his words are growing more faint, falling away in the space between us.

Brian's hands are on my shoulders, and I realize that he is helping to lower me back onto a sleeping mat. I'm outside myself, aware that I'm fading into sleep but powerless to stop it. The world dissolves into blackness, and I float into it.

I wake again in a fully illuminated cave. The pounding in my head has dimmed, but I still wince at the brightness of the light. I see now that I'm in a shallow, cave-like living space with a low table, shelves, and bed that's entirely carved into the rock. I rub my hand against the stone, and find it wonderfully cool, despite the heat emanating from the mouth of the cave.

I rise slowly, paying attention to my body. I'm stiff and sore from sleeping for so long, and my temples throb slightly at the movement, but otherwise I'm fine. I stand slowly and stretch my body out before walking into the sunlight, and to the mouth of the cave. The heat hits me like a wall as I move closer to it, and I shield my eyes from the brightness.

As my vision adjusts, I see that the cave opens onto the valley floor of a crevasse. The walls rise sharply on either side, with only a short stretch of land between them that slopes gently downward. Small cave openings line the opposite wall, some at ground level and others accessed with ladders cut into the stone. In the center of the expanse between the walls is a massive hole in the ground with a metal lift built onto one side. It's clearly designed to hold large groups of people.

To the side of the hole is a giant, flat craft. There's an angular, enclosed pilot's box at one end, and gold railings around the sides. The center of the craft is covered in a cornucopia of food—fresh fruit, roasted meat, and steaming bread on a long table covered in a shade awning. As I watch, people funnel from the lift covered in dirt and queue calmly at the craft. From here, they all look young and vibrant, not one of them is bent with age or has gray hair. Armed guards, dressed just like the ones that knocked me out, let them on and they each pile heaping plates of food, many of them retreating into the caves that line the base of the crevasse.

I catch sight of someone waving to me, and find that Brian is walking towards me from the craft, expertly balancing two plates of food in his other arm. When a faint breeze blows the smell of the feast in my direction, my stomach comes alive.

"You're looking better already, but I'm betting you have a fierce hunger," Brian calls out to me, smiling.

He finishes climbing the slight grade up to the cave, hands me one of the plates, and motions me back into the shade and coolness of the cave. We sit down at the stone-cut table. It's at the perfect height for sitting cross-legged, and undercut so I can squeeze close. The plate he gave me is loaded with bread, cheese, a leg of chicken, and a small dish of fruit. For a second I'm caught out without the cutlery I've grown accustomed to, but when I see Brian start in with his hands I give into it. *How posh I've become living with the rich.*

"How're you feeling? They expect you to start work tomorrow. Think you can?" Brian says through a mouth full of food.

I have no idea what the work entails, but I'm certain I can handle it. "Much better, thanks to you. I'll be fine to start tomorrow, can I continue to sleep in this cave?"

Brian shrugs. "If you want. Ain't no one here putting flags down, so if you want something different just find an empty one."

"Brian, how many are there in this mine?"

He pauses, doing some quick mental calculations. "'Round thirty I believe. We had more mind you, but guards didn't take kindly to them trying to get free."

"How long ago was this?"

He shrugs, and then pauses and looks into my eyes. Anger simmers there, some hidden pain, and a wisdom that only comes with age. "Time doesn't have meaning here, you'll figure that out quick."

He goes back to eating, and I stare at his tanned, youthful skin. There's something happening here that I haven't figured out yet.

"I'm shocked they give such good food here," I say, digging into the chicken leg.

"Like I was saying, it isn't so bad here and we get three squares a day, just the work is hard and you're expected to do it. And we can't leave, there's that too."

His plate finished, Brian leans back against the wall behind him. He grabs a pouch from his hip, and pulls out a small pinch of green leaves. It's pungent, earthy and sweet, and the smell fills the small space of the cave. He puts the pile in his mouth and chews it, closing his eyes and savoring it.

"What's that you're eating?"

"Same thing I gave you yesterday, helps calm the body and mind. Once you get used to it, doesn't affect you so much." He smiles at this, laughing internally at the reaction I had to it yesterday. "Grows all over down here, everyone eats it."

Brian appraises my clean plate as I finish the last of the succulent fruit. "If you're done eating, let's go get something to drink. I'm thirsty and sure you are too."

Brian rises and grabs his plate, so I do the same and follow him out of the cave. We walk down the slope, and as I look around the crevasse I notice others leaving caves and doing the same. We follow the slope down to the flat craft. One of the guards is still there, lounging on a deck chair and watching the scene through half-lidded eyes, his helmet removed. He idly sips from a canteen. Up close I can see his glistening black armor, and the strange, long silver tube strapped to his waist. It ends in a handle similar to a melter, something meant to be pointed and shot then. *Maybe that's the sonic cannon they shot me with.* I shudder at the memory, and feel nervous that he'll hassle me, but he doesn't even look in my direction.

Others are filtering onto the craft behind us, and they stare at me openly, or nod quietly in greeting. Up close, I see that they're all around the same age as Brian, and equally well built. Every one of them looks healthy and strong. We wash our plates in a bin, and grab two canteens from the end of the table. I follow Brian from the craft and we walk to a raised stone circle. The other guard sits on the edge of it, drinking from a canteen, his attention on the steep wall of the crevasse. *They're barely watching anyone here.*

As we approach the raised circle, at the center is an open maw that sinks into blackness below. It's my first time seeing one, but I realize that this must be a well. From the side of it sticks a spigot, and I follow Brian in using the manual pump to fill my canteen. The entire time the guard ignores our presence, and those that funnel in behind us. I pause for a moment and follow his gaze up the wall of the crevasse. It's nearly a hundred feet of sheer, unblemished rock all the way to the top. It would be impossible to scale.

As I'm watching the edge, I just catch sight of a black blur as it darts between tree cover, and I can't help but smile at the sight. *Good boy, Charon.* The guard notices nothing, and sips again from his canteen as he stares at the cliff.

"Water here is good and fine, treated by the palace. That isn't a real well, just a cistern they fill up every few cycles," Brian says as we retreat from the spigot.

The sun blazes overhead, the midday heat is sweltering. I'm sweating just from the short walk outside, and my headache returns. I drink greedily from the canteen as we walk back to the cave, my eyes squinted against the sunlight.

"I didn't expect how well you're treated here; ample food, water, and a break during the day—"

"You just can't leave is all. And you got to work, there isn't opting out of that. Palace gives us a production quota, but the mine is healthy and it's not a great stretch."

"What is it you mine here?" I ask, as we reach the mouth of the cave.

"You'll see tomorrow lad, there's some explaining to do on that one. I'm due back in the hole now," Brian says, and smiles at me.

He turns and walks back down the slope, and joins the others that are making their way to the lift. They swell onto it, perfectly orchestrated, and descend into the darkness below.

Did he just call me lad? We're basically the same age. I shake my head and retreat into the cave, and out of the heat of the day.

I spend the afternoon thinking over what I've learned so far, and wondering at a way out of this pit. As the sun starts to fade, I walk the length of the crevasse. I'd guess it's around a mile long, and it tapers to a sharp point on either end with the mine set in the center. From above, I imagine it looks like a rudimentary eye, with every side a sheer cliff.

Weeds grow along the length of the wall, and even sprout from small openings in the rock itself. I smell them, and find they're the same as what Brian ate earlier. I pick them as I go, and stuff them into my now empty canteen until it's full. The opening is just wide enough that I can put two fingers in and pull the weeds back out.

As I'm leaving one end of the crevasse to go back to my cave, I hear a rustle in the leaves above me. I look upwards, and just make out two glinting eyes in the coming darkness. I smile deeply at the friendly face far above me.

"Charon, I'm fine, starting to have a plan on how to get out. Are you safe?" I say into the cliff face, and it echoes upwards.

"*Yes, fine.*" His words carry down to me. Faint, but unmistakable. I miss him already.

"Stay that way, and meet me here tomorrow night after the guards leave." As I turn, I catch sight of a glowing ship on the horizon. "I have to leave now. Goodbye, friend."

I run back to my cave, and make the entrance as the ship crests the top of the crevasse, and starts the descent down to the ground. There's a mountain of food at its center. Faint tremors vibrate up through my feet as the lift hauls people up from the pit. Tomorrow, I'll be with them.

NINE

DOROTHY

The palace paints a bleached stain on the flattened top of the hill. Around it, the thick forest has been clear-cut in every direction. It's obvious the intended effect is one of awe—a startling white structure rising out of an otherwise uninterrupted sea of trees. It only reminds me of humanity's hubris. To inhabit an alien landscape and create something so foreign to it gives me a clear idea of what to expect from the king.

As we get closer the grandness of the structure comes into view. The palace is a great, hulking thing built in angular forms and jutting terraces, surrounded by a sea of white. An expansive swimming pool sits behind the structure, lit majestically by the now setting sun. As we start to descend I spot others lounging at the side or swimming idly. They wave up to us as we pass like a strange summertime fantasy. Sophia and I stare down at them from the railing, not returning the gesture.

The ship navigates to a landing pad adjacent to the pool where others like it sit in a line. Below us, people in gleaming black armor shuffle around between the ships, one of which is loaded with a table of food. As we descend, it raises up and leaves in perfect synchronicity, angling away from the palace in a direction different than we came in. I watch it until the view is blocked by the palace, and wonder where it's heading.

On the flight, the rush of wind was too loud to allow for conversation, and I'm grateful. There was a time when I could play the part. I spent years with a smile as a mask, trying to win people over to my political agenda. After weeks alone in the Cosmos though, even the thought of a conversation with this many people is exhausting. Especially people like these. They seem carved off from the Sun Gate I knew. They're content to stand in small groups talking into each other's ears and sneaking furtive glances at us. As the craft slowly descends, the din of conversation grows again, and the same woman from before approaches me.

"Please, come with me and I'll show you both to your quarters. I believe you'll want a bath and fresh clothing before meeting the king. Unfortunately, we do not have a charging station for your machine."

I start to correct her that she is not *my machine*, and likely has more brains than half those on this ship, but a slight nudge from Sophia stops me. As much as I want to deny it to myself, my body yearns at the thought of a bath and fresh clothes. *How long has it been?* Just thinking about it, my skin breaks out with the itch of dried sweat, and I smell myself again. Looking down,

I notice again the tears that cover the athletic clothing I left our city in, and laugh out loud.

"Yes, that would be wonderful. I didn't ask before, but what's your name?"

Her blue eyes meet mine, and in them I see a sudden, fierce intelligence. The corner of her mouth tugs upwards in an ironic grin. "Dorothy Sungate," she says, and bows her blonde head slightly.

I stare at her in shock. *It's just a name, it means nothing. It has to mean something. Names always mean something. Is she like me? Are we related somehow?* I search her, looking for similarities then. Blonde hair, blue eyes, pale skin, rail thin. She's nothing like me. She looks up again, her eyes meeting mine, and lets out a small laugh.

"I'm sorry, I have you at a disadvantage. It must be a surprise for you to meet someone with the same name, but I've known it was possible for some time," she says as the ship touches down. A ramp extends from the side, and Sophia and I follow her down it. I think the others funnel off behind us, but I'm not paying them any attention.

"Are we..?"

"Related? Not that I'm aware of. It's more of a coincidence, or maybe some kind of cosmic joke."

I turn to study her again, but she keeps her face pointed forward and expressionless. She leads us towards the palace. The gleaming white we saw in the distance is from marble tiles that seem to glimmer in the setting sun. Their construction is flawless, with barely a seam visible between the perfectly cut squares, and the pattern stretches across the entire grounds in straight lines. It looks insane, detached from reality. I had no idea this much marble existed anywhere.

"So then, are my friends here?" *Or did the Narrator lie to me?*

She looks back at me, brows furrowed. "Friends? We've no other guests here, are there others you traveled with?"

"Wait, how did you know my name then?"

She pauses in her walk and studies me, considering something. Then she shrugs and keeps walking. "It will be clear soon."

I turn to Sophia, walking at my side, and arch an eyebrow. She shakes her head, not understanding this either. We follow this new Dorothy to the side of the palace. *I can't call her that, it's too strange...she seems more like a Dee.* The same white marble tiles cover its walls, and the trim is covered in gold leaf. It's gaudy and ostentatious, like a child's dream of being rich.

Dee takes us to a side door. It spans well above our heads, even dwarfing Sophia. It swings open noiselessly, and as tall as the door is, the ceiling yawns further above it. The hallway we walk into feels cavernous. Thick, red carpet blankets the hallway, and the walls are covered in mismatched art. It feels like several collections were jumbled together and then hung on the walls without regard to history, period, or even art style. *Tasteless.*

As we walk down the hall I think over what I've learned. These people knew I was coming, hell, they knew my name, but they didn't seem to know exactly when I would arrive. That wasn't a welcome party I encountered, they weren't out there waiting for me. The Narrator didn't exactly say that Nick and Charon were here either, but that they were trapped by a "gleaming white mystery that never grows old." He was definitely trying to point me in this direction, for whatever reason. *Did he orchestrate this whole thing? Is he the king? What's his game?*

I'm so lost in thought that when Dee stops to show us into our room, I nearly walk into her. Sophia grabs my shoulder from behind and saves me the embarrassment. She opens a door on the left side of the hall, and we follow her in.

The room is dominated by a window opposite from the door. It spans the entire length of the room, and gives an incredible view over the colorful tree tops. In the distance, the city juts upward from the canopy. The room itself resembles the rest of the palace—white marble tile covers the floors and walls. Gaudy and cold. A large bed is set on one side of the room, and opposite that is a door leading to a private bath.

"I hope you find this to your satisfaction. There are some fresh clothes in the closet that are your size. Dinner is in two hours. I'll come and get you," Dee says from the doorway. Then she bows slightly, turns and shuts the door behind her as she leaves.

Sophia stands in the room in silence for a few moments, unmoving as we take it in.

"She locked the door, didn't she?" I ask, already knowing the answer. *Whatever is happening here, they either don't want us to leave, or don't want us to explore.*

"She did." Sophia walks into the room and sits down in a thickly cushioned, red armchair that is positioned to look out the window. Her chest cavity retracts, and she reaches inside to pull out a worn, leatherbound book that would fit well in my palm. The absurdity of her giant, metal frame in the small chair reading the hand-sized book makes me burst out in laughter.

Sophia glances back at me and shrugs. "We might as well relax while we can."

She doesn't have to remind me again.

I let myself sink below the surface of the water, let it embrace me, smother me, and then surface for air. The tub is long enough for me to stretch out, and carved completely from white marble. *How long since I last bathed?* That's a question I never had in my old life. And it does feel like my old life here.

It's strange that only a couple of weeks have passed since I left the city. I feel changed, like I'm waking up from some dream. The memories of it all belong to a different person. I couldn't possibly have done the things that I know I did. I close my eyes and images of the Skyball surface, people screaming as gas kills them, and Nick nearly dying in my arms. The scene shifts to Nick's face as I tranquilize him, as he understands fully what I've done. In my memory, his face transitions quickly from grief to acceptance, as if he always expected me to betray him. And the reasoning I did all those things feels so distant now that they just look like the actions of a monster. *Am I a monster?*

I slip under the water again, blocking the outside world, and shake my head to clear the memories. *I did what had to be done. The problems of our city just all seem so much smaller now that I've seen other cities. That's normal.*

With my eyes closed, I feel the water around me. The weight and warmth of it covers me, caressing every corner. I smooth the tension from my skin, I push the past from my thoughts. I run my hands down my arms, the curves of my breasts, the softness of my stomach, the round of my hips. I massage the tension from my muscles. I clean myself, washing away the dirt and easing the weight of memories. They're the only things left to remind me I was once unclean.

When I finally get out of the water my skin is pruned and whitened. I dry myself, and put on a plush red robe. Next to the bath is the thin, black armor that Nick gave me so long ago. I grab it, swirl it in the suds of the tub water, scrub the inside with my hands, and hang it to dry. *No idea when I'll get a chance to do that again.*

I find Sophia reading in the same position. The setting sun glances in through the window now, backlighting her. The gold leaf of the title, *The Library of Babel*, shimmers against the black, bound leather. Memories swirl around me of a different time, of a different Sophia. I decide to embrace them, and sit in the light at her feet.

"Will you read to me, Sophia?"

She glances down at me and nods. I close my eyes and let my mind drift to a time when I listened to a different Sophia read. I smile at the memory.

In the story she tells me of a library that contains books with every combination of letters to have ever existed, and in doing so also contains every story ever written. But most people only ever find books of nonsense, the letters thrown together haphazardly and not forming a single thought. Those that study the texts slowly die or go crazy looking for a single one with meaning. I see the parallel in our own lives, most of us living events like a random jumble of letters until our books end. I realize how rare a truly good story is, then.

Sophia stops reading, and I open my eyes and look up at her.

"Dorothy, I have been curious. Why did you name me Sophia? You said I reminded you of someone, was it your mother?"

Where do I start to answer that?

"I...my mother died when I was very young. From cancer. She hid it from me and my father, so when we finally did learn of it, she was nearly dead already."

"Did your city not have a disease transfer machine? I thought all cities came with them."

"We did, but my mother refused to use it. In our city, it caused the subjugation of an entire caste of society—"

"I think that was actually one of the intentions of it, to create a clear societal hierarchy," Sophia says, nodding.

"Right, well my mother didn't agree with that. She would get sick, and my father would humor her and hire a doctor. But she knew that he would force her to use it if he found out about her cancer. So she hid it until it was too late, until there wasn't enough time to find someone to trade with her."

Sophia says nothing, but watches me and listens.

"After she died, it was only my father and I for a while. He tried to raise me, but the things he's good at aren't exactly what a child needs to know." *Swordplay, science, and an incredible lack of compassion.* "So he hired me a governess, Sophia. She was from one of the lower castes, but came from a family of book sellers. Her main love was reading, and my family had a massive library.

"So every day after my lessons, we'd retire to the library. She'd pick one of her favorite books from our shelves, and read stories to me. She showed me magic, and romance. She read me classics, fairy tales, and fables from all throughout history. I loved those days with her."

"So when you saw me reading, it reminded you of her?"

"Yes, well and you both have a motherly way about you. Something I guess I've always felt I missed out on in my life."

She nods at this. "What happened to Sophia?"

The pain at her question is sharp, but before I can respond there's a loud knock from the door, and I'm snapped out of my reverie. Both our heads turn in that direction.

"Please be prepared for dinner in half an hour," A courteous male voice says from outside the door. I listen for more, but I only hear his footsteps retreating down the hall.

I look down at my now dry bathrobe, and stand. I brush the weight of memory from my shoulders and focus on the night ahead. "I guess I should get ready."

Sophia nods to me, and returns to reading her book.

Dee's right that the clothes in the closet of my room were all my size. After taming my hair with a brush, I find a loose, cream-colored cashmere dress that ends just above my knees and put it on. It's the only one with a tasteful neckline, and grabs lovingly to the highlights of my curves. The rest of the dresses seem tailored to show off more than they cover. When I look in the mirror, I recognize it. This is a different color of the same dress that I wore the first time I met Nick. *How did they know my size and preferences?*

Another knock at the door pulls me back from the memory. I hear it unlock and see Dee, wearing the same dress as mine, but several sizes smaller and in a dark blue that highlights her eyes. Dee blanches when she sees, but I laugh throatily.

"I guess we have more in common than a name," I say.

She colors slightly, and I wonder what she's thinking. "I'd been wondering if something like this might happen. Of course, I can change—"

"Please, don't. If anything it makes me feel like I have a friend tonight."

Dee smiles at this, and offers her arm to me. I take it in mine, and we walk down the hall, deeper into the palace. *I'm drawn to trust her. Should I be? Is this just from the confluence of our names?*

"Will your machine be okay to stay in the room?"

I think she'll be more than happy. "Yes, it will be fine," I say, careful to use the pronouns that Dee expects.

"So I understand that you can visit other cities as a traveler, but why did you leave your own?"

So they don't know everything, then.

"Well, in my city, a friend and I stopped our disease transfer machine, and turned it into something that cured all diseases. I'm guessing that your city had one of these machines?" Dee nods in response, so I continue. "To do that, we had to infiltrate the Medical Authority tower. We were targeted as a threat by our city after that, and it sent machines after us. So we fled."

After a contemplative silence, she asks, "What was your intention in changing the disease transfer machine?" I can tell it's not an idle question, there's something she's trying to understand. As we talk, she navigates us down another hallway that should take us closer to the center of the building.

"It was unjust and caused the suffering of an entire sect of our society. It was completely inhumane. It had to end. I tried other ways to change things, but not many in our city wanted it to change. So we had to force our way," I say with passion edging into my voice.

Dee nods at this with a wry, knowing smile. "It sounds like we do have much more in common than a name, then. I did the same in our city." I turn and study her intently. "I was able to convince people here, but I had to use a rather unfortunate strand of logic."

"And what was that?"

"That it was the only thing that would let us live separate from the lower castes," she says, and lowers her eyes. There's pain in her eyes. *She precipitated something she didn't intend. Cured one evil, to spawn a whole new breed.*

We reach the end of the hallway. Dee stops us in front of a set of giant, wooden double doors. They swing open as we approach. The room on the other side is expansive, and decorated for a cocktail party. Tall, mahogany tables litter the landscape. On the left of the room is an antique piano, and music drifts up beautifully as a man plays it. On the right, is a raised dais set in front of an ostentatiously large bay window. A white marble throne sits on it.

As we enter, a sea of cocktail dresses and suit jackets swivel to observe us. Everyone here is young and beautiful, I still don't see a single person older than I am. They all look around the same age. The conversation dims, and then dies altogether. From the silent crowd, a man steps forward. He's taller than I am, blonde, and there's something familiar in the way he holds himself. He has a bold chin, thick eyebrows, and high cheekbones. *A conqueror's face,* I think warily. He's wearing a dinner jacket that's dazzled with gold trim, and on his head sits a white marble crown. He approaches us, and Dee separates her arm from mine and steps to the side in deference.

From my side, Dee says, "Dorothy, may I present King Allen Cloudspire."

A pit opens up in my stomach at the words.

TEN

NICHOLAS

All around me is darkness. If not for the cool rush of air against my face and the thrumming that travels up through my feet and into my legs, I would think I was somehow back in the Cosmos. We left the surface and the rising sun just moments ago, but any evidence of that light disappears nearly instantly. As my eyes adjust, I notice a soft blue light beneath the lift. We race downwards to meet it. It grows until the world around me is bathed in blue hues. Everyone's skin looks sickly and their eyes like hollow, black pits.

And just as quickly as the world above disappeared, a new one appears around us. It seems to pop into existence all at once as the lift exits the tunnel, and enters the cave beneath. It's tall, maybe half a mile at its peak, and shaped like a rounded dome. As I squint at the cave floor, I find tunnels leaving in multiple directions. The walls are covered in luminescent blue stones that shimmer and light the darkness. When the lift finally comes to a stop, I notice mine carts on tracks that are stacked tall with the blue rocks.

As people start to shuffle off of the lift, Brian comes up beside me.

"It's a wonder, isn't it? We might be stuck working this mine, but at least it's beautiful."

I nod, dimly, still looking up in awe at the luminescent walls around us. "What is this glowing rock, Brian?"

He shrugs, and walks towards the exit from the lift. I follow, and we step down onto the hard cave floor.

"They call it Indigo. No one rightly knows if it ever had another name, it wasn't something we'd seen before. No one knows why it glows either, there isn't a source to it. You break it apart and try to find the glow inside, but it isn't there. Just smaller and smaller pieces, and they all glow. It's why we mine though. Palace requires a *steady supply*."

"What do they use it for, do you know?"

He turns to me, and grins devilishly. In the blue hued light it looks maniacal, dangerous, and I unconsciously shrink back from him.

"You haven't guessed yet? You notice how we all look the same age?" He laughs suddenly, viciously. It's a noise made of sharp-edged steel that barely conceals the anger behind it. "I don't even know how old I am anymore. This rock, it's the fountain of youth! Keeps us all young and healthy, so we can work this mine for eternity!"

"What do you mean, the fountain of youth?"

He shrugs again, and turns away from me. "Palace turns it into something that stops aging, reverses it even. They give it to us infrequently, any more than that and we'd keep getting younger."

I stare at him in the darkness, one of the mysteries falling into place, only to be replaced by another. *The fountain of youth? What the hell is this stuff?*

"Come on, time now for working. We can chat while we mine, unless you get too tired." He chuckles to himself.

I follow Brian to a pile of tools. He grabs out a pick and tosses it in my direction. It's heavy in my hands, and I know already that I'll be sore from swinging it. He grabs another for himself, and walks towards one of the myriad tunnels that surround us. I follow him.

"That is a plasma pick, it'll only glow as you swing it. Cuts into the rock like butter, but it'll still wear you out to swing it. Work slow, be smart. Doesn't do anyone good to have you worn out. When we get a rock out, we'll work together to chop it up. Then we've got to haul it out of this tunnel, bit by bit."

We walk into the tunnel. It's over ten feet in diameter and lined with the glowing, blue rock. Up close, I can see that they're partially translucent like quartz, and like Brian said, the glow seems to come from every inch of them. We walk deeper and deeper into the tunnel until we hit a place where there are no more rocks. The darkness ahead is deep and impenetrable.

"We work these tunnels backwards so we don't have to walk through the dark. I'm not scared of much now, but no one wants to travel through that pitch. Let's start on this one, here." Brian says, motioning to a hunk of rock the size of my torso embedded in the rock.

We take up on either side of it, and alternate our swings. There's a rhythm to it, a flow, and we both work to it. With each strike, a flash of blue light comes from the end of the pick that cleaves through the rock. We chip layer by layer back around the Indigo until we have to split sections off of it to continue. Each piece we remove we carry back to the mouth of the tunnel where an empty mine cart waits. I feel the weight of the work in my shoulders and back already, and know the strain will spread from there to my chest, hips, and thighs until it covers my entire body. It's not fatiguing yet, but it will be soon.

The air in the mines is naturally cool. On the descent it felt cold, but now as the sweat beads on our skin it feels like a welcome reprieve. The air is completely still, but with each swing from Brian's pick a rush of air blasts over me and dries my skin. And so we find a stasis point in the work, a sustainable balance of pick strikes, rock hauling, breathing in, and drinking from the canteens at our hips that we filled at breakfast.

My muscles are just starting to feel tight when a loud buzzer sounds from the main cavern. I pause in my strikes and turn to Brian, a questioning look on my face.

"That's lunch, then," he says, grinning, and slings his pick over his shoulder.

From the darkness, we emerge. Dust-covered and sweat-stained in our workwear, the lift raises us back into the sunlight. A jumpsuit was delivered for me by the guards at breakfast, and the clean fabric looked out of place amongst the miners. Now I fit in. As we breach into the sun, the smell of food is visceral, like an assault of complexity after the dusty mine air, and I can feel the hunger that's building in the miners around me like a tidal wave.

The same as it was the day before, a large, flat craft has landed next to the lift. The center of it is covered in a variety of food. *A moveable feast.* We all filter off the lift towards it, and a line forms peacefully and naturally. In front of me is a youthful blonde woman, her hair pulled back into twin ponytails that fall on each shoulder. She stands a head shorter than me, and when she turns around her eyes are like two flecks of blue ice.

"Brian told us that you come from a far away city, but I've only ever heard of this city here. How far away is it?" she asks. Her voice has a musical, childlike lilt to it.

I smile back at her, wondering how to explain. "I think you wouldn't believe me if I told you." Her brows furrow up at me, frustrated at my non-answer, so I continue. "At the top of your city is a door, and if you have the right key it will let you travel between every other city. There are thousands of them, but they're spread out across the galaxy impossibly far apart. That door links them together in some higher dimension. It's a strange place."

She stares at me for a moment, and then laughs uproariously. "It's good to have another storyteller. Living here, I've learned to prefer fantasy. It's always so much more fun that way. I'm Josephine by the way."

She shoots her hand out to me, and I stare at it, and then back to her. I see a little girl from my city, an innocent little thing that's growing up without a father now, and I wonder if she still wears her hair the same way. I wonder if she stopped working for Allen's family, like I told her to. I imagine her free, and living outside the city, and it breaks my heart with happiness. I take Jospehine's hand in mine like a man on a sinking ship.

"Mister, why're you crying? Was it something I said?"

"You just reminded me of someone very dear to me." I say, wiping my eyes. Josephine smiles sadly at me, and then grabs a plate from the buffet and starts to her lunch. I follow suit behind her.

When the day is finally over, Brian and I take our dinner back to the cave. My body is exhausted from the work in the mine. At any moment, I think I'll drop my plate of food and fall asleep on the ground. But there are things to talk about tonight, and I still have to meet Charon before I let myself sleep. When we reach the cave, I slump down onto the carved stone floor and start to eat mechanically.

"Work's hard, eh? You'll get used to it quick," Brian says.

I nod, focusing my thoughts. I think I'm understanding most of this world, but there is a piece missing.

"I was wondering, where are the children, Brian? Surely a group of this size couples off? I haven't seen anyone younger since I came through the city nearby."

Brian arches an eyebrow at the question, and then laughs. "You're a quick study, boy. Keen of you to notice that. Mind, it took us a few years to figure that same thing out. That drink I told you they were making from Indigo? Nearest we can reason it makes us sterile. Not sure if it's the men, or the women, or both. But sure enough we haven't had a kid in this mine, and there's been plenty of tryin'." He winks conspiratorially at this, and chuckles.

It's like a puzzle piece falling into place. The soft treatment from the guards, the abundance of food, even allowing me to not work while I recovered. *They need these miners, and they can't replace them, or at least not easily.* I think back to the city I came through, to Jasmine and Ash, and think how enticing fresh blood would be. But with the city's defenses, it would be suicide for anyone to try.

"So the city nearby, they've never been exposed to Indigo? When I came through, I saw both the young and the old there."

Brian nods in response. "They don't leave their sanctuary, and King Allen isn't going to give it to them otherwise. Not sure they want it though, to be fair."

I nearly spew food out of my mouth. "King who?" A pit opens in the bottom of my stomach.

"King Allen Cloudspire, senior mind you, there's a prince with the same name."

In the fading light, I stare at Brian in disbelief. There's no trace of the sleepiness that threatened to overwhelm me moments ago. My heart thrums hard in my chest, adrenaline coursing through me. *Allen Cloudspire is king? This repetition of names, it's not a coincidence. This has to be the Narrator's hand at work, somehow. It's not safe for us here, we're too linked to this story already. I have to get out of this pit mine and find Dotty.*

"Brian, if I told you that I have an idea to break us all out of here, what would you say to that?"

His frown is quick and deep. "I'd say someone with your name already died trying that, and he took others with him. People aren't happy being stuck here, but they're comfortable and safe. If we did try to escape, they'd just kill us all."

"I think if you all left, there might be safety in that. How many mines do you think there are?"

Brian shrugs. "No way to tell, but we've never seen ships flying elsewhere overhead."

"It's a gamble, but if this is one of the only mines, and population numbers can't increase, and they can't get people from the city, then you're all irreplaceable. I think that's why the guards treat you okay, why there's so much food and water for you."

Brian opens his mouth to protest, but from the furrowing of his brows I can tell I've caught his full attention. "I can't rightly speak for the people here, but I don't think anyone is interested in an armed struggle with the guards. Even just the two of them. Whether or not they need us, a few are likely to get killed in the shuffle."

I nod, and walk to my bed roll. From behind the pillow, I pull my canteen from the night before, and unscrew the cap. A pungent, earthy smell immediately fills the room, and turning back to Brian I show him that the canteen is full of the weeds that grow along the crevasse. His eyes search mine questioningly.

"When you gave me this stuff, and I'd never been exposed to it, I was asleep in minutes. Now, you all chew this stuff regularly, and it barely affects you. But I'm betting those guards don't, and they drink from the same cistern as the rest of you. If we wait for it to get low, and then sink this into it, they'll pass out and we can take their craft to escape."

"Now, that's actually a clever idea," Brian says, and grins deeply.

"Do you know how long until the cistern will be refilled?"

"Can't be much more than a few more cycles, water's starting to have some sediment in it."

"Good, can you talk to the others? See if we're all in agreement?"

"Aye, I'll talk to them. You think you can fly one of those things?"

"Not a clue, Brian. But to me, it's worth a try."

He grins at that and shakes his head. Then he grabs my dishes to take them back down the hill. A large chunk of chicken remains, and I grab it and set it on the table. Brian arches his eyebrow at the move.

"A midnight snack, I'll get hungry."

He nods and leaves the cave at that.

The day slides towards darkness, and as the sun leaves us, finally so do the guards. I wait for the caves to quiet. Sleep pulls at my eyes, and with every fiber I want to give into it. But I can't let it take me. Not yet. As the final shades of daylight wink out, twin moons appear in the new darkness, and light everything in their eerie glow. I slide from the cave, carrying my treat for Charon.

Slowly, quietly, I make my way to the edge of the crevasse. The camp is silent now, people have found their homes for the night and are resting. For a moment I try to imagine how long this same cycle has repeated, these same moments again and again, unending. I imagine what not aging and being stuck in this endless loop of work would be like. *The only sign of progress they have is the changing mine.*

When I finally reach the edge, I peer upwards into the darkness. Two eyes shine like gems in the void.

"Charon, I brought some chicken for you."

I throw the meat as hard as I can towards his eyes in the darkness. Pain lances through my overworked muscles at the sudden motion, but I hear it land far above me, and Charon's eyes disappear as he hunts it. The sounds of his eating echoes quietly down the cliff wall.

"Have you been able to find anything to eat up there?"

"Just fruit," his voice purrs back to me.

It pains me to think of him starving on a diet of only fruit. I imagine him wasting away while I eat my fill from a buffet three times daily.

"I'll bring more tomorrow night, I'm sorry boy. I have a plan for us to steal the guard's ship, but it may be several cycles before we can still. Do you think you can get down here?"

"Yes. Not too steep. Only in daylight."

"Okay, once we knock the guards out, we can steal the ship and escape to the city."

"Dotty?"

"Finding Dotty? I haven't figured that part out yet."

He doesn't respond, but even in the darkness I can sense his concern.

"It'll be okay, boy, we're not leaving here without her. Stay safe, I'll find you again tomorrow night."

And with that, I make my way back to my cave to finally give myself over to sleep.

ELEVEN

DOROTHY

The evening swirls around me in a flurry of cocktail dresses, clinking glasses, and micro-food on platters. If I ignore the faces, and the white marble everywhere, the scene could be lifted directly from my own city. Piano music layers over polite laughter and the boasting of men and women.

"I have so many questions for you, but I'm a better man than to exhaust a guest, so I'll stay focused. Is our world strange to you?" King Allen asks me, refocusing my attention.

We sit together on the edge of the party at a small marble table with an army of attendants and guards only paces away. One of them walks forward and deposits a crystal tumbler of whiskey for each of us, and then retreats. It reminds me of nights at Allen's house, of time spent sipping whiskey in their family garden. It reminds me of the Allen that existed before Nick. It feels like a far distant past.

"Only in how familiar it all is. How is it that you expected my arrival?"

"Ah, it's not so mysterious is it? The Narrator told me a long time ago that you would visit our world," the king says, and smiles.

"The Narrator? How do you know him?" *How did he tell him a long time ago? It couldn't have been more than a few weeks since I left our city.*

"The current state of our world begins with that man, or whatever he is. He came to me years ago—"

The king trails off as a man impetuously makes his way through the room towards us, nearly pushing others out of his way. He has the same bold chin and thick eyebrows, but his face is softer and younger. His matching gold-lined dinner jacket can barely contain the muscle that swells underneath it. Around his neck hangs a pendant of white marble. He approaches us and bows to the king, but when his eyes meet mine he colors slightly.

"Father, you sent for me?"

"Yes. Dorothy, I want to introduce my son, Prince Allen. He is much better at entertaining than an old man who likes to sit, drink whiskey, and talk about mutual friends."

An old man? He's no older than I am. How the hell does he have a son that's nearly the same age?

"A pleasure," the prince says to me, bowing again in my direction.

"My boy, I was just starting to explain the history of our world. But I fear from me it would sound boastful. You're much better suited to tell it. Would you give our guest a tour of the palace, and fill in the details?"

"Of course, father. Dorothy, please come with me."

I stand and nod to the king, then follow the prince as he cuts a path through the throngs of revelers. He walks like a peacock, chest held high and chin jutting upwards. The crowd parts for him, and it's clear he expects them to. Their conversations turning to whispers after we pass. *Well, this is causing a stir.* When we reach the far side of the room, opposite of where I entered, two attendants open the wide double doors so we can pass through. On the other side, a long white marble hallway stretches into the distance.

Prince Allen basks in the impressiveness of the hall for a moment, a moment of reflection that seems entirely curated for me.

"The palace is impressive, don't you think?" he says, not turning to look at my reaction.

"It is very white."

"Yes, one of the first abundances we found on this planet was marble. My father had it extracted because he had the vision to build a monument."

He talks about his father with a nearly religious exaltation.

After saying this, Allen starts slowly forward down the hall, and I follow beside him.

"Before our city was opened, my father told me that he had been given a vision of the outside world. My father is in no way a religious man, so it was a strange claim from him. He told me that there existed a new natural resource that would change all of our lives."

"Did he tell you how he had this vision?" *Or who gave it to him?*

"He never told me the details of the vision. I see it now as the first of his miracles." I blanch at the word. "When Dorothy, our Dorothy that is, convinced the council to change the disease transfer machine, she was elected as the person to enter the control room." He swallows hard at this. "Thankfully, she wasn't harmed, but one of the outcomes was that the city sprawled open."

So, she's also met the Narrator then.

"My father immediately led an expedition into the jungle. The men that went with him told me he seemed to know exactly where to head. My father led them into a cave, and there they discovered Indigo."

"Indigo?"

"A mineral native to this planet that has several strange...properties." Allen turns to me and smiles viciously.

The hallway ends in front of us at a door that's different from the rest. It's a single polished metal plate with an access panel mounted to the wall in front of it. Allen rests his hand on the panel, and the door slides noiselessly open. Behind it, a spiral staircase descends. I follow Allen into the passage.

Gone now is the ostentatious marble and plush carpeting, replaced entirely by functional austerity. The stairs, walls, and ceiling are formed from a black metal that's lit by occasional sconces. It gives the eerie impression of sinking into a dark cave that expands in every direction. Pipes mounted to the ceiling follow the stairwell downwards, our only connection to the world above.

"This was the start of my father's second miracle. He brought back an abundance of the mineral, so much that others doubted his sanity. A few others led expeditions into the planet at this time, but only returned with some native fruit. Most were still content to live as they were, inside the walls of the city."

I can barely restrain laughter at the way he talks about his father. But I stifle it, and keep listening.

"My father went to work with the minerals, and very soon had distilled it into a drink. He's no chemist, but as I watched him work in his newly constructed lab, he seemed to work like he'd been given instructions on what to do. He told me that the drink reversed aging, and named it Indigo after the rock that gave it birth."

As we descend further, a strange blue glow starts to grow at the end of the hallway.

"And it worked? That's an incredible creation, if so." *Is that how everyone I met is the same age? The Narrator said, "A gleaming white mystery that never grows old." Is this what he meant?*

"It worked exceptionally well. For the first several months, no one believed him. Then the effects were undeniable, and people clamored for access. My father set a monumental price, and when people could no longer afford to pay for the monthly doses, he demanded their fealty instead.

"You may be thinking from this that my father is a greedy man, but he was also magnanimous. For those in the lower quarters whose money was insufficient and fealty was not useful, my father offered them access if they worked for him. Some of them work in the palace, while others *more suited* were sent to the mines my father created."

In my head, I see how the same castes of society were carried from inside of the city to outside of it. *Order must be maintained.* Again, something the Narrator said nags at me. *"A practice common / From birth to the stars beyond / Of men over men."*

The blue glow intensifies until everything swims in it. It drowns out the feeble light from the sconces on the wall.

"So this thing your father created has to be taken continuously? A constant supply of this rock is required? Is this what your miners extract?"

"That's correct. We only have one mine operational now, it's near the site where my father originally found Indigo. Our other mines supplied the marble for this palace, as well as much of the metal needed to build this facility."

"What happens if the supply stops?" *Or the miners decide they don't want to continue working?*

Allen shrugs lightly, as if the possibility can't be taken too seriously. "My father believes a cascade of cell mutation and rapid aging will occur eventually, but no one really knows for sure. It's not a concern though, the miners' contracts don't allow them to quit working."

There it is. The shit that props this whole world up. It's always there, if you dig deep enough. "So the miners are kept alive by this forever drink your father made, and aren't allowed to quit working. And even if they did, they'd likely die soon after. So you keep them as slaves?"

"We do not keep slaves, I find that statement very offensive," Allen responds haughtily, looking over to me with furrowed brows. "They are indentured workers, nothing more, fulfilling terms of a contract that they agreed to. They benefit from this and are treated well."

Why is it that the powerful always try to keep the moral high ground?

I'm about to respond when we step out of the spiraling stairwell, and into the massive expanse of a factory. Everything is awash in neon blue light. It seems to glow organically from every surface. As my eyes adjust to the sight, I see the illumination is from bits of translucent rock that are in various forms of processing across the room.

On one side, giant boulders are being unloaded from a mine cart. On the opposite side, a vat of glowing blue liquid is agitated by an automated paddle wheel. In between these two extremes are machines that crush, pummel, and grind the rocks into a fine powder, and then combine them with more ingredients into the final liquid form. Workers are scattered across the factory floor—monitoring equipment, holding clipboards, and assisting in loading raw material. They all wear white lab coats and face coverings.

I follow Allen into the room, and I'm stunned into silence. The factory flows like clockwork around us. The workers give a slight nod to the prince as they pass, but otherwise ignore our presence. The machines here are loud, but not overly so. They operate smoothly, efficiently, and I'm drawn into their repetitive motions. After one machine crushes boulders, another actuates immediately behind it and continues to refine the material down to a powder. I'd read of factories before, but never experienced one.

I follow the processing line and see the powder added to a clear liquid in measured doses. It glows faintly. Another liquid solution is carefully titrated in, and when the perfect balance is hit, the mixture glows heavily. From there it's boiled and condensed several times, removing impurities. In a flash of memory, I see myself working similar tools to create terrible concoctions. I'm no chemical genius, the methods were all captured in my father's books. But I made something truly terrible, and I gave it to monsters. Memories of the night at Skyball circle in my head. The screaming, the blood. The death.

I become aware that Prince Allen is speaking at some point. "…line was built from my father's vision after we moved into the palace to automate a large portion of production. Of course, with such high demand this was necessary. As you can see, the factory runs smoothly, cleanly, and creates a steady stream of Indigo. We are not wanting here."

"Why are you showing me all this?" I ask, but it hits me before he responds. *To impress me, to intrigue me, to make me stay.* I can tell my question has caught him off-guard, it's more honest than he expected.

"To show you what our world has to offer," he responds after a pause, and blushes slightly.

"Cart returning soon!" The call goes up around the room as a red light starts to flash. It draws both of our attention.

In the corner of the factory, technicians hurriedly clear the mine cart's track of debris and tools used for lifting boulders. The job done, one of them presses a button on the wall, and the mine cart rockets off through the darkness. We both stare after it for several moments.

Allen turns then and like we're twin moths drawn to a flame, we walk over to the glowing blue vat of fluid. I watch as a mixing paddle turns slowly through it. It's still translucent, but only just barely.

"I bet you've seen curious things in your travels through different cities, but nothing as curious as this," he says with a charming smile, his composure regained.

On a nearby table there's a graduated cylinder of the liquid that looks left over from some testing. It pulls to me, calls to me, promises the end of death. *What an incredible thing it would be to live forever.* I never thought I was overly interested in my own mortality, until the possibility of removing the barrier was presented to me. *It's tempting. No death, no pain, just unending comfort. But this is all built on the backs of others. Just like our city, it's beautiful on the surface. But underneath that exterior, it's skewed, ugly.*

I think again of the Narrator, of his goals in sending me here. In creating a temptation for me that pits my own nature against my morality. *This is all a test. A moral proving ground. A fucking story.* And with that thought, my anger returns. It does not flare and die, it blazes into being like an active volcano, ready to spew magma and hate. I see the miners who toil to create this life, and though I've never met them, their plight makes my chest ache. Cursed to live forever as a slave, so these people can enjoy fine dining and cocktail parties every day. *It's no different than our city. The setting changes, but the rules don't.*

"I've seen many abuses of people in my travels, but certainly nothing as great as this. You've built a world on the backs of others and framed it as a great achievement. Only here, people can't even get freedom from death. I can only imagine the horror of their existence. I would like to return to my room now."

I say it slowly, my words dripping in venom, and with each sentence, Allen's face gets more flushed with anger. I see his hands twitch, and wait for him to try and strike me. *Let him try, I'm not defenseless, I know how to fight.* I curl my fists and watch his body for clues.

Instead, he relaxes, his face calming back to his princely superiority. He calls over my shoulder, deeper into the room, "Guards, remove this guest to her room, she's being difficult."

I turn, and only then do I realize that two bodyguards have followed us down into the factory. They must have moved silently behind us. One of them points a long, shining gun toward me. Absurdly, I notice how the shimmering blue of the room dances over its surface as the world around me seems to slow. I try to move sideways to avoid it, but a wall of pressure hits me suddenly and my balance evaporates. My legs turn soft as I lunge, and I strike the floor hard.

I try to move on the ground, to crawl to my feet, to get away, but nothing seems to work right. My head swims, and I puke from a violent wave of nausea.

Allen bends down at my side. "I can be sweet too, I promise, but I can also be sour. I won't tolerate insolence. What you're feeling will fade, but let the memory be a reminder that you are in my world. You will not disrespect me."

With that, the guards grab my arms and haul me to my feet. Vertigo washes over me, and I puke on myself again. I hear them mutter in disgust behind their reflective, black helmets. And then mercifully, I pass out.

I come to as they drag me back through the cocktail party, but I can barely lift my head. Around me I hear the stir of conversation die, and in the hush of the room whispered threads drift to me.

"...girl didn't know her place."

"An absolute mess..."

"Poor thing..."

"... only want her for her womb anyways."

"...prince needs an heir..."

The words float around in my head without meaning. I turn them over, inspecting them like an alien puzzle. The guards stop and when I open my eyes there are a pair of feet in front of my downward gaze. With great effort I raise my head and see Dee, her face flushed in anger. *Why is she so upset,* I wonder distantly.

"I see the prince still has not learned how to treat a woman. What a disgrace. Give her to me, I will help her back to her room," she says haughtily.

Muttering, the guards lift me and Dee loops my arm around her neck. Without a care that my vomit stains her clothes, she pulls me to her. I'm shocked at the strength of the smaller woman as she supports me, and find then that my legs have started to respond to my brain again. With her help, despite my mounting nausea, I hobble from the room and back down the hall to my quarters.

A feeling of floating, of weightlessness. I drift upward into Sophia's arms. I smile drunkenly into my friend's blank face, until I see the skewed reflection of my own in the metal and grimace at the sight. With the world spinning again, I close my eyes.

"What happened to her?"

"Sonic cannon, it disrupts the inner ear. No lasting damage, but she needs to rest. The prince..." Dee trails off.

I fly over to the bed in her arms, and feel its welcoming presence envelope me as Sophia sets me down. She removes my stained clothes, cleans my face with a soft cloth, and covers me in thick blankets. The darkness tugs at me again, but before I go, I rummage through the conversations I heard earlier. I see everything as a puzzle piece, and I feel their edges to determine the shape of what's missing. Everyone's the same age, but the prince is younger. They all drink the forever drink. There are no children here that I've seen, no sounds of their playing, no toys fit for them. The king...the prince...dynasty building. *The prince needs an heir.*

The outline of the missing shape forms in my head, and I realize that its edges are my edges. Disgust washes over me. I am a salvation the Narrator promised them. I am their future, their hope of growth. My rage simmers. *I will destroy them.*

I let sleep take me.

A dream of anger and fire. I scream in eternal frustration, and as my rage washes over, it all burns down. The city I came from, the structures. And in the flames I see the people I love burned with it. I see my mother who preferred death to participation, I see Sophia, my caretaker, who preferred me to life. I see Nick running from the flames as they try to swallow him. As I try to swallow him. I see hundreds of people in the Skyball, they stare at me with blank gazes, unmoving as the fire takes them.

I see a vat of iridescent blue, its contents being slowly stirred. The liquid calls to me, but the desire only fuels my endless, boundless, seething anger. And when I scream again, I will the fire to take it. To burn it all down. To end another world.

TWELVE

NICHOLAS

Days pass at the mine. There is a natural tide to their flow that can only come from the repetition of doing the same things. With each cycle, I rise for breakfast stiff and sore. I work each day with Brian, and every night I bring Charon food. I watch the cistern slowly dip lower at every meal. I can taste the sediment in it now, like sand against my throat when I swallow, just as Brian said I would.

On the lift to and from the mine, I plead my case to the others in quiet whispers. Not for just my sake, but for all of ours. Some nod along, others tut in disapproval. There's fear of reprisal, and also a fear of what will happen when they stop taking Indigo. But under that fear is an anger that simmers in all of them. There's a hunger for freedom, and with each passing day there is more hope in their eyes.

"I watched the guards pilot that flyer yesterday, it seems mostly automated. There was one control lever for take off, and then I'd guess the other must be for movement. I think it auto-balances though," Henry Fiveboroughs tells me as we descend for an evening shift.

My father was friends with a Henry Fiveboroughs, and when I look into the miner's blue eyes, I wonder if he shares the same affable nature.

"Good work confirming that, Henry. Did you see how they accessed the pilot's cabin?"

He shrugs. "There's a hand scanner, but only keyed to them. Guessing we'll need to drag 'em there once they're out cold."

"Do you really think the strength of the weeds will be enough to knock them out?" Jospehine asks, concerned.

This particular point has come up several times, and we've chased it around. Some are convinced that it will, some are concerned that it will be strong enough to even knock the tolerant amongst us out. Others are unsure. It seems the effect is not the same on everyone, even between the tolerant there's a wide range of dosage used. And of course, some plants are stronger than others. We spent an entire lift ride discussing where I harvested them from, to know if they were predominantly shade-grown or sun-grown, to earmark their potency.

"Those cats don't have any experience with the stuff, Joe, we just gotta be careful to not have too much ourselves," Brian responds, and shoots me a conspiratorial wink.

I've been dosing myself heavily the last few days to boost my tolerance, but I still know I'm at a disadvantage. If I'm not careful, I'll wind up knocked out like the guards and have to hope the miners execute on the plan.

"How long until we put the dose in, then? Is the cistern low enough?" I ask, after a brief moment of silence.

The miners look at each other, judging the depth from their own experiences these last few days. There's agreement in their faces as they turn to each other, My pulse quickens in response.

"We drop it in tonight, let it soak and see what happens in the morning. Or we lose our chance for a long time. They'll surely fill it up tomorrow evening," Brian says to me, others nodding in agreement.

"Any opposed?" I ask, my heart pounding in my throat.

There's complete silence. The weight of finality descends onto my shoulders, and I hope that I haven't just signed everyone's death sentence. When we reach the bottom of the mine, everyone filters off. Just another day, nothing has changed. *I hope this works.*

Brian shakes me from my contemplation when he thrusts a pick into my hands.

After night falls, I pull my cosmic armor out from under my bedding. My clothes I brought here were too ragged to save, but the thin barrier underneath them was still in good shape. It saved my life twice now, once when Charon and I battled a room full of Inquisitors, and then again when Edward tried to stab me. I might need it again tomorrow, and it won't be noticed under my workwear. I quickly pull it on.

While I'm alone in my cave I also check the functionality of my wrist knife. My gift from Micah, so long ago. *He had a better idea of where my story would head than I did.* Even though the guards must have searched me for weapons when they brought me here, the cloaking of the small plasma knife means it avoided detection. I haven't wanted to show it to the miners, in case it gives them a different idea of me. When I pull my wrist back, it springs upwards and coats the inside of the cave walls in a celestial blue glow. I quickly snap my wrist forward again, hoping that no one saw the light.

Memories burn my conscience long after the glow of it fades. With my eyes closed, I watch the blade pierce Edward's chin and leave him a charred husk. In a time that feels ancient now, I see a Plague Doctor impaled with it. I shudder, and hope that tomorrow doesn't bring a need for it. I'll defend myself and my friends, but I'm tired of killing.

Lastly, I grab my canteen from under my pillow. I uncap it, and the room is instantly full of the dense, earthy aroma of the sleep weeds from the crevasse. Time in the heat of the canteen has made them start to decompose, and I can only hope that it doesn't affect their potency. I wrench the cap back on quickly, my heart thudding at what comes next.

The night sky lights my path down to the cistern from the cave. I wished we were completely obscured, but this world seems to have little cloud cover, and the phase of the twin moons seems nearly constant. In the soft light, I make out the shape of Brian crouched next to the well. I make my way slowly down the hill to join him, careful to avoid making excess noise.

One of the major flaws in my plan, that both Brian and I have recognized in the past few days, is a complete lack of knowledge on what surveillance there is on this encampment. It seems unlikely with the level of technology the guards have, and the value of these miners, that there would be none. But despite careful checking, neither of us have seen any evidence. Still, we do what we can to prevent being noticed.

We work quickly, our actions already discussed while we worked in the mine that evening. Brian takes a thin rope made from scraps of old jumpsuits, and ties it to the neck of the canteen. He leaves the cap barely engaged at the end of its threads while I hold it out over the cistern. He gives the rope a few careful tugs, and when our eyes meet in the dark, he gives me a quiet nod.

The plan is to have the cap hold the rope onto the canteen so we can slowly lower it to the bottom. Once the canteen is near the water's edge, a quick snap of the line will break both it and the cap free. With Brian's nod being the signal for me to release the canteen so that he can start lowering it, I let go. And then I watch our plan fail spectacularly.

As soon as I release my grip, the weight of the canteen on the threads causes it to rotate slightly and dislodge. Seeing that the canteen is about to fall into the water far below, both Brian and I throw our hands out to grab it. They collide into each other, and then into the canteen, throwing it into the side of the cistern with a loud, resonating *CLANG*. Brian and I duck down, and listen to the container ricochet around the walls on its freefall down. It lands in the water below with a splash, and then everything is quiet again. I nearly laugh from the ridiculousness of it, but the potential consequences are too real.

Brian and I crouch next to the well, barely daring to breathe, and wait for the world to crash down around us. Time dilates, and in my panic I latch onto each night noise as the coming of the guards. But as the stillness of the night descends again, and the time stretches longer, our tensions ease. Brian reaches out to me and grabs my shoulder, and gives me another solemn nod in the darkness. He carefully moves away from the well, and I watch as he travels quietly back up the grass slope to his cave. *It's started, we'll see what happens next.*

I go to find Charon afterwards. I'm quieter than I've ever been sneaking to the edge of the mine, tray of leftover food in hand. I can feel the fatigue from the day, from all my days here, resting on my shoulders. But an excited nervousness drives me forward. I pay attention to every noise and rustle on the way.

"Charon, are you there?"

I'm about to call out again when I hear a weak response from above me. "*Yes, hungry.*"

I'm immediately stabbed by guilt at the thought of my friend starving. I've been bringing him food daily, but only what I can stow away without drawing attention. Like on previous nights, I carefully throw what I've brought to the top of the cliff wall. I hear him immediately tear into it, and then the night grows quiet again.

"This is the last night Charon, we make our move tomorrow. I've poisoned the well, it should knock the guards out. Can you come down here in the morning? Then you can feast."

"*Okay.*"

There's so much more I want to say. To tell him that I miss him, that I'm excited to leave this place, that I'm sorry for how hard this has been. But the distance and darkness between us makes it all sound strange in my head. I find myself yearning for our days of exploring the Cosmos together, just the two of us.

"I'm sorry friend, we'll be out of here soon," I say into the dark. Charon gives me a slight growl in acknowledgement, and it makes my spirit soar.

I shield my eyes against the morning sun as I watch the flyer come in. Every moment feels laced with potential. The flat bottom of the craft catches the sunlight as it starts its descent, and forces me to look away. I look around the camp, and see every other miner outside of their caves watching the craft. *We look too interested.*

I start the walk to the center of the camp, just as I have on other mornings. If this is successful, maybe I can take the flyer back to the palace after we leave all the miners at the city. Maybe I can use it to rescue Dotty. I'm still so far from my goal, but for the first time since I came to the mine, there's a glimmer of hope.

As the ship descends and I get a glimpse of the top of the craft, that hope immediately sours. Every food delivery there have been two guards. One stays on the ship while the other stays near the well. This morning, there are four of them, one steering the ship downwards and the other three poised at the railing. *Do they know?* My heart sinks further when I notice they don't carry their usual Sonic Cannons, the long gleaming silver guns have been replaced by something much shorter and blacker. Something whose devastation I know too well. *Melters. Fuck.*

They spot me in the same instant, all three visors snap downwards and stare at me. In unison, the guards step down from the flyer and plummet the final distance to the ground. Before they land, small jets on their boots kick on and slow their fall. The whole scene is clouded in dust and dirt, and I hear some of the other miners scream as they seek cover back in their homes. *There's no sense in running, there's nowhere to run to.*

I think through my options, but I can't see a single way that I take on three guards armed with melters and survive. My armor wouldn't survive it, and my wrist knife feels incredibly inadequate here. Through the dust, the three come for me, melters raised. I feel a defeat so crushing that I can only stand there, shoulders slumped, and wait for what comes next.

At least they only seem interested in me. Maybe they'll leave the others alone. I had to try something. I hope Charon will be okay.

"Get on your knees, fucker!" the one to my right screams, and I comply with my hands raised.

The miners are staring at me from around the encampment now. They're in the mouths of caves, or paused on the hill down to the craft. Their eyes catch mine, and then shoot down in shame. *They've got the right of it. This was my plan, no one else needs to bear the consequences.*

The pilot's cockpit slides open as the guards shuffle closer and hem me in, guns still raised. Their bodies obscure my view, but

I hear footsteps crunching on the dirt as they approach us. The guards part, and a man with golden hair and a proudly jutting chin stares disdainfully down at me. His armor is golden, but he's foregone the helmet the guards keep on. A chain hangs around his neck, a single pendant of white marble.

He meets my eyes and he sighs dramatically. "You must be Nicholas Fiveboroughs. The one from this world was a pain also, had you heard that?"

I stare up at him, my eyebrows furrowing in confusion. "How do you know my name?"

He laughs deeply, but there's no mirth in it. "We heard your story from the Narrator." I flinch at the name. "And you can call me *Prince* Allen Cloudspire, I believe you're familiar with the name?"

I stare at him, mind swirling, and he laughs again.

"The Narrator told us he likes to keep our names the same from city to city—he likes the *storytelling opportunity*. We're not actually related of course, and you were never really Allen Cloudspire anyway. How fitting it is that you've come to a new city and wound up right back in the dirt, where you belong." His laugh rings out again, then he kneels down in front of me. As he does, the guards tighten their perimeter until they're all just a few paces away.

I glower into his blue eyes. "How did you know I was here?"

"The guards told me they picked someone up outside the city recently, so we reviewed the camera footage." He points up to the cliff wall above me, and my stomach sinks. *Do they know everything?* "It was fairly easy to piece together when Dorothy started asking if we'd seen her *friends*."

"Dorothy, she's at the palace? Is she safe?"

"Oh yes, quite safe. I need her to be, she's the only woman with a working womb here, everyone else had too much Indigo. Besides those cretins in the city, but they're not of good stock anyways. I'd be likely to catch a disease dipping into that well. The Narrator was quite clear, too. *'For your legacy to be immortalized, seek the one from beyond these skies, Dorothy Sungate is your eternal prize.'* Old man loves speaking in damn riddles, but he's been right about everything else.

"Now, she's not my first pick, if we're being honest chap. That one's got quite a fiery temper, and she's a bit broad, a bit too muscular. I prefer my women more docile, more respectful. Then again, maybe she will be after bearing a few children. It's not like I can't have others on the side anyways." He stands and shrugs, indifferent to the anger that's flushed my face.

I understand the monstrosity finally. *The Narrator told them we were coming, and lured Dotty to the palace. Their family lineage can't continue without heirs. That's the final power here, the final thing they can claim. They want to be the only family to make children in this hell.* It's so petty, so stupid, that I'm momentarily stunned by the banality of it. Dotty and I are the breakers of shackles, the walkers of the Cosmos, we have seen things that this prince can't imagine and it's all brought us to here, to this moment. To this current nightmare. We went through all of this just for her to be held as an unwilling bride, and me to be killed. Rage soars inside me, that great blossoming tyrant of passion, and as the prince turns to walk away, I lunge for his back.

He's outside the ring of guards now, but I almost have him. Then a steely grip grabs me on either arm and stops my progress. I struggle against it, trying to free myself, but the guards hold me firm. The third steps up behind me, and the cool metal of a melter rests against the back of my head.

The prince turns back around at the noise, and gives me an exhausted expression. "Don't kill him just yet, my father wants to interrogate him. He might have information that will help us. Bind him for now, we still need to let the cattle eat." Turning back to the miners he screams, "What are you looking at, slaves! There's your fucking breakfast, start eating and get to work." Then, turning back to the guards he adds, "I'm thirsty, is this water here safe to drink?"

"Yes sir, although the cistern is low so it may taste like dirt," One of them responds.

I smile, despite it all. Knowing that I'll still just as likely die later, but now there's a small glimmer of hope in my chest. *They have no clue about the well. Maybe, just maybe.*

The guard behind me removes the melter, and wrenches my arms behind my back. Cool metal straps circle my wrist, and cinch shut.

"Prisoner secured," he says, and the other two let go of my arms and step back. "I'm thirsty too, watch him." He steps around them and I watch him follow the prince onto the flyer to grab a canteen.

"What are you smiling at, rat?" the guard to my right says, and then punches me squarely in the face.

I fall onto the ground, my bound hands pinned underneath me. But the pain of the punch barely registers. I shift my body to watch as the prince and one of the guards step over to the cistern and fill their canteens. They take long, greedy gulps, completely unaware of the chance they've given me. A grin spreads across my face, and I taste the blood that's streaming from my nose.

A vibration grows in the earth, and then comes the familiar sound it always carries as it draws near. As the noise rises and drowns out the morning, everyone's attention shifts. I can't see the pit from behind the guard's bodies, but I know it so well there's no need. The lift is returning from the mine. It's returning from a mine that should be empty. From the pitch. It will crest the top of the mine shaft at any moment.

It gives me the opportunity I need. When the guards turn around to see who or what rides the lift, I carefully position my bound wrists, and angle my hand backward to extend my hidden plasma knife. I feel it rip into my other arm, and as the smell of roasting flesh drifts upwards from behind me, the grip of the bonds loosens.

I tear my arms apart, and rise up behind the guards. There is a fury inside of me. A rage at this world, at all the worlds that live on the backs of their own people. A hatred for those that would keep slaves. That use and use and use so that a few can live more comfortably than the rest. I rise up in time to see the occupants of the lift come into view. And with a face covered in blood, I smile.

THIRTEEN

DOROTHY

I jolt awake in a darkened room, confused where I am. My head aches, and there's the lingering taste of vomit in my mouth. I see the outlines of the White Palace around me, and my thoughts start to find form and coalesce again. Finding out this world is built on slaves, being put down by Allen's guards for objecting, hearing his true need for me as I was dragged back to my room. A hatred, dulled by sleep, burns in my chest again.

Another world, propped up by pillars of injustice. Just another iteration of people using people. How many are built this way? Is this all we're capable of? I'm filled with a rage so visceral that I want to tear myself apart, just to see something broken. I stare at the blank expanse of white ceiling, and seethe. *I will break this fucking world, and every other world like this.*

Sophia appears at the bedside and sets a glass on the small table next to me, breaking me from my budding wrath. "Good morning. Here is some water, take it slowly so it stays down. They used something on you that disrupted your equilibrium."

I nod, and sit up to take the glass. I sip the water slowly. It washes the foul taste from my mouth and eases my headache. It cools my resentment, if only momentarily. Sophia sits on the edge of the bed, and the frame sags under her great weight.

"Dorothy, the one from this world, told me only that you angered the prince when she brought you back here. What happened?" she asks after letting me finish my water.

Slowly, I explain the previous night to Sophia. I tell her about the king, and the prince, and how they knew to expect me from the Narrator. I tell her about Indigo, and how it shaped this world. About the processing facility underneath the palace, and the mines that feed it. And the slaves that sustain it all, that are bound to work those mines forever. It's an incredible sounding story, but Sophia nods along.

"But why bring you here? Why are they so interested in you?"

I pause, thinking through what I heard last night.

"I think, I think Indigo must do something to disrupt fertility. The prince hasn't taken it yet, he's younger than the rest of them. I think they want me because I can give the prince an heir, and cement their family's rule. His father wants to show that they can have what the other immortals can't. As they dragged me through the ballroom last night, I heard as much."

Sophia pauses and stares across the room, her shoulders slumped. "This place is beautiful, but rotten. We need to find a way to escape."

"I know, but I won't leave until we find Nick and Charon, and we don't know where they are. I won't abandon them."

"Feed this hungry world / A freedom so long foreign / To find them again," Sophia responds quietly with the Narrator's words.

Of course, he told us everything. "He must have been referencing the slaves, there are a few in the palace, but most of them mine Indigo. So does that mean we can find Nick with the miners? The prince told me there's only one operational mine left."

Sophia gestures towards the door. "We are locked in this room. We have to solve that problem first. While you were gone, I confirmed that the door has a sturdy metal core, I cannot break it down without drawing attention."

As if in response, a knock comes from the door. We both fixate on it, and I get out of bed on legs that are still shaky, and walk to it.

"Who is it?"

"Food delivery. Step back from the door."

We both remain seated. The door swings open to reveal a guard, the long, slender tube of a sonic cannon held against his chest. He marches into the room and steps to the side, allowing a diminutive man in a white chef's jacket behind him to push a cart into the room. The waiter meets my eyes for a moment, frowns, and then busies himself removing covers from the cart.

The smell of eggs and hollandaise sauce, carried on an undercurrent of freshly baked bread, fills the small space. As angry as I am, my stomach growls in response.

"Food service occurs twice a day. Do not attempt to leave this room." The guard says when the other man has finished preparing the cart of food.

At a motion from the guard's hand, the waiter exits the room first. He keeps his gaze fixed on the floor. The guard files out behind him, the door clicking softly shut behind them both. In the silence after they leave, Sophia and I stare at the door.

Once I regain my feet, I pass that first day of confinement vibrating with anger. I pace the room, the walls feeling smaller with each passing hour. I tear the room apart, looking for hidden cameras and listening devices, and find nothing. I spend long stretches of time listening for movement at our door, or staring out the glass window into the surrounding forest, wondering what's happening outside. In contrast, Sophia sinks more into her quiet contemplation. She reads and pauses to think, absorbed entirely in her book.

When the knock comes for my second meal of the day, it catches me pacing.

"Food delivery. Step back from the door."

I move to the other side of the room and join Sophia near the bay windows. When the guard enters he catches my wild eyes, and his grip tightens on his weapon. The same scene from the morning plays out, but this time the smells of meat and vegetables pervades our small space. I'm surprised to find my stomach growling.

When the guard and waiter exit the room again, Sophia places a cool metal hand on my shoulder.

"Calm yourself, we may be here for some time."

I bristle. I've never been confined before, never been locked in a cell. "We could overpower that guard easily."

"Yes, true. And then what will we do? We need a plan, and to do so we need to be mentally focused. Please, get some food and come sit with me."

I exhale deeply, and follow her advice. The food here is marvelous, something I hate to admit. Cutlets of chicken are arranged on one plate with perfectly browned skin. Next to it, a fresh salad, full of nuts and various lettuces. A smaller plate holds roasted potatoes. I'm reminded for a moment that the chefs who made this are kept as indentured servants, and have the momentary urge to throw the whole thing to the ground. I breathe through my fury, and after assembling a plate, pull a chair over to sit with Sophia.

While I eat, and stare across the darkening tree tops, Sophia pulls a new book from her chest cavity. *Slaughterhouse Five* is embossed on the cover in gold leaf. The sun sets, ripping the sky apart in oranges and purples, and in that fading light, a wind blows over the treetops. I watch the twin moons rise over this strange world, and she reads to me.

It's an unusual, fragmented story of a man lost in time. The specifics are hard to grasp. The book references a world I don't know, historical events that I've never heard of, an alien species that seems fabricated. I'm set adrift, searching for landmarks through a sea of trauma, until Sophia reads the phrase; '*Everything was beautiful, and nothing hurt*', and I see it for what it is. It's a pretty lie, just like the palace around me.

These beautiful marble walls, this life of grandeur and glamour, it's built on the backs of others. The people here have closed their eyes to it, they focus only on the grandness, on the endless present, fixed in time and unchanging. They are shielded from the mine, from that view of slavery that supports their lifestyle. My thoughts race to the facility underneath the palace. To that iridescent blue vat. To a mine cart returning. And then, my thoughts stop.

Maybe that's a way to break this world. Maybe that's a way out.

"I think I know how we can get to the mines, actually," I say.

Sophia stops reading, and turns to look at me. In the reflection of my face on hers, I'm smiling.

Days pass in the same sequence of events. Breakfast is delivered. I train calisthenics to stay sharp, and then shower off. Sophia reads to me, and eventually dinner is delivered. It's monotonous, like the same day played over again. Until the cycle breaks.

One night after I've eaten, I hear the door unlock again when it shouldn't. It swings open slightly and Dee glides into the room. She's wearing black tights and a form-fitting top now, and sneaks a furtive glance behind her into the hallway before shutting the door again silently. Then she turns to me.

Whatever she was going to say lodges in her throat. She stares at me for a moment, cocks her head, and smiles. I'm sitting on the floor as Sophia reads to me, and I feel strangely like she's intruding on something private.

"Is your machine reading to you?"

Sophia moves to put the book away, but I reach out and lay my hand on her wrist. "She is, Sophia loves books, and as it turns out, I love being read to."

"Sophia?" A confused look spreads across Dee's face.

Sophia turns to her. "That is the name Dorothy gave me, when she discovered that I was self-aware."

Dee's eyebrows arch upwards, and a grin spreads across her face. "That's incredible!" Then, as if remembering why she came to the room, the grin disappears. "I would love to know more, but I came here with a more serious mission. We've got to get you both out of here. Have you figured out their plans for you?"

I stare at her for a moment. The concerns of their world seem so far away after being locked in this room for several days.

"I overheard some of the guests at the party. They want me to produce an heir for the prince?"

Dee colors in shame and looks down. "That's it. I've tried for years to convince the prince to not pursue it, tried to make him see that it's not a just course of action, but he only listens to his father. He's more like him with every passing year." Her eyes come back up to meet mine. "Look, this isn't a good place, if you haven't figured that out. We're stuck in time and commit the same sins every day to keep it that way. If you stay here, it will destroy you. I'm afraid it's already destroyed me."

From behind her back she pulls a long, flat object and offers it to me. After a moment, I realize that it's the plasma blade I brought with me to this world. The one I took from Nick so long ago. I stand and grab it from her. The heft of it feels like a decision already made.

"Will you leave the door unlocked for us?"

"Yes, but there are sentries all over, even this early in the day. They carry the sonic cannons that you've already experienced, but also melters. The king wouldn't want you killed, but they'll certainly use them and beg forgiveness later. Usually they heavily guard the palace and only barely patrol the ships outside. It seems the prince is planning something though, and it's drawn several of them out to the landing pad, so stealing a ship is impossible. It will make it easier to navigate the palace, but even if we get you outside to the forest, you'll almost certainly run into a trap in the woods. I don't know how you'll escape. I came tonight hoping you had figured out a plan."

I look at Sophia beside me, and she gives me a slight nod in agreement. "Who has access to the facility under the Palace?"

Dee gives me a questioning glance, and then seems to understand my intent. "But the mines aren't a way out, you'll be stuck there—"

"With my friends that I've been searching for, hopefully. I'm not leaving here without them, and like you said, I doubt that we'll be able to fight our way through to stealing a ship anyways."

She considers for a moment. "If you time it right, there is a ship that delivers meals three times a day to the mines. It will be guarded, but not heavily."

I smile wickedly as the final element of the plan clicks into place. "Perfect, thank you. But, who has access to the facility? I saw the prince use a hand scanner to open it."

"I do," she says, and mirrors my smile perfectly.

I arch my eyebrows at her, questioning.

"There was a time, right after the city opened and before Indigo, before this damn palace, that the prince and I were a couple. We were so young then, just children really. He still trusts me from those days."

We move quietly through the hall. I follow Dee, and Sophia follows me. With the long expanse of openness it would be easy to spot us, so we cling to the right side wall, and pause to listen near every door frame we pass. The corridor extends in front of us, and then turns at a sharp angle before the doors that lead to the main ballroom.

We listen for the soft muffle of footsteps on the carpet, but hear nothing. And so we slowly inch down the hallway. My eyes are focused on the corner as I try to absorb every little sound. Move forward. Pause. Listen. Move forward. Pause. Listen. As we get closer to the bend, we hear a barely audible conversation from around the corner.

Dee holds up her hand for us to stop, then turns around and mouths *get ready*. I wipe the sweat from my hands on the black tights I found in the closet of my room, and draw my plasma sword from the holster. I turn to see Sophia crouched, her hands formed into sharp, metal points. I crouch down as well. When the guards round this corner, their gaze will be lifted and scanning the hall. They won't be prepared for an attack to come from down low.

Before we left the safety of our room, I put back on the cosmic armor that Nick gave me. It's a comfort underneath my clothes, but I know it won't stop a melter. At this range it would tear through me, and the lingering plasma from the shot would quickly eat through whatever remained of my body. They were almost non-existent in our city; beyond that antique Nick used against Cerberus, I'd only seen images of them. The risk of causing damage to the walls was too high, but I've read enough about them to know the effect. Thankfully, the guards should only have one shot before they need to recharge them.

I watch as Dee circles back behind us and grabs the handle to the nearest door. There is a faint click of the latch. She opens the door wide, and then forcefully slams it shut. After so much time in silence, I flinch from the sudden noise. Around the corner, I hear the conversation stop immediately. And then, barely audibly, I hear soft footsteps as they move down the corridor towards the bend.

In the pause before violence, images of my father teaching me to use the plasma sword come up unbidden. Swordplay had no practicality in Sun Gate, but the hobbies of the rich barely ever do. So from a young age we practiced, drilled, and trained. He taught me forms, and then taught me that none of them mattered. Winning mattered. Survival mattered. *"Be what they don't expect, don't be a textbook,"* he'd say. He taught me that quick brutality ended most fights, and surprise attacks were always preferable.

When I came for his biolock, before Nick and I stormed the Medical Authority, I used everything he taught me. He knew what I wanted only in the moments before the plasma sword cut through his wrist. When I sprang from around a corner like this and separated it from him with surgical precision, I saw the expected surprise in his eyes, but also unabashed pride. I left him there after, tied to a chair with a cauterized wrist. We were so different, but maybe more the same than I'll ever have the time to understand.

The steps are drawing near to the corner. I tighten my grip on the handle until it hurts, and wait for the moment. The pain sharpens my focus, and the fear and anticipation brings a peaceful clarity to the moment. *There is only this moment, and then the next, and then the next.* I tense the rest of my muscles for the attack. *Be what they don't expect*, I tell myself.

When the first guard's foot comes into view, I strike. In a great rush, I carry my momentum forward and up through the blade in an arc that leaves a blue blur on my retinas. It takes him from the outside hip and up through his collarbone. He didn't even have his melter raised, but carried it against his chest. My sword cuts through it all and leaves two pieces of everything behind. There is the momentary spray of arterial blood, but the wound cauterizes nearly instantly and fills the hallways with the smell of smoked flesh.

Their training becomes clear immediately afterwards. The second guard goes into action as soon as he sees my plasma sword, and everything slows. He throws himself backwards from the corner, and starts to level his melter. My sword is still raised from the opening strike. I planned to flow through them both swiftly, but he's deftly moved outside of my reach. *I can't reach him in time, he's too far.* I tense my thighs to leap toward him, but as I get my sword in position to strike, I see he's already brought his melter up. *Fuck, I'm too late.*

I know I won't make it in time, I can already feel the bite of the melter, but the momentum is there and all I can do is follow it. I'm dimly aware of a rush of silver beside me as I prepare to lunge. It blazes by me, and throws me off balance. I ram into the wall to my right as a shot from the melter blazes over my left shoulder, and burns a hole through the palace.

When my vision steadies, Sophia has speared the guard with her great, pointed hands. They both enter through his chest, puncturing his lungs. Only a bloody gurgle escapes his lips as he tries to scream. Blood pours down over her hands, and then sprays the hall as she rips them outward.

She saved me. For a moment, I imagine the shot took her and there's a pain in my chest that I haven't felt in years. Memories of my Sophia, my friend and teacher, flood me, until Dee shakes me from it.

"We have to move, now!" she yells while shaking my shoulder, and I'm brought back to the present moment.

Blood and viscera cover the hallway like a bizarre painting, and the smell of roasted flesh hangs in the air. The second guard still twitches out his final moments on the ground, but the first is already losing color. As my head clears from the fight, I hear the palace around us coming alive with movement. There are faint shouts from other rooms and I can just hear the sound of running feet. Dee bends to grab the second guard's melter off the ground, and we run.

Caution forgotten, the three of us sprint down the hall and burst through the main ballroom doors. They swing wide to a new scene. A long table that bisects the room is being prepared for breakfast, and servers are scattered across the room at work. Their heads snap to us as we rush through the doors. I don't know if it's the weapons we carry, or the sight of Sophia covered in dripping blood, but they run immediately.

We don't even break our pace to observe them. I'm only dimly aware of their terrified screaming. Dee takes the lead and sprints toward the table. She jumps onto it, and back down the other side. Sophia and I follow suit right behind her. Two towers of champagne flutes, positioned at either end of the table, come crashing down from the shake of our passing. *If the guards don't know where we are already, they'll just have to follow the noise.* We push onward to the double doors on the other side of the ballroom. In my mind I'm mapping the route the prince took me on to the entrance to the facility. *We're not far now.*

There's a moment that I have hope here. A flash where I see things work out perfectly. We evade the guards, we blast through the double doors in front of us and find the hall empty, we make it to the lab beneath our feet without further incident. We escape together, unharmed.

Dee gets to the door first and slams her shoulder into it, melter raised. It swings open and we all spew into the adjoining hallway, and then freeze. In front of us are six guards, their melters all pointing towards us. In the middle of them is the king, dressed in a marble white sleeping gown.

"Come now, didn't you think this was a little predictable? Our mutual friend visited and told me to expect this, but I didn't need to hear it from him. I posted guards here and at the exits. What a delight that I chose the right one to attend this morning. Of course our traveler would try to escape after her treatment, that's only natural. That I expected. Although, I must say I'm disappointed you chose to help them, Dorothy." He sighs deeply, and I glance sidelong at Dee to see her frown tighten. Her melter is pointed down slightly, and I can see from the glowing bar on the side that it's still charging from the last shot.

"I've lived so long in this monstrosity you created that I started to lose sight of who I was. She reminded me of that, reminded me of how I used to be," Dee says, and smiles sadly. "This world isn't right. You're not right. Living forever isn't right. I helped you prop up this world on an endless cycle of injustice, and I can't take it anymore. I don't regret trying to help her, I only hope that she can escape and change things, make them right."

Some part of me knows what will happen next. I want to pause time and save Dee, stop her, but in her sad smile I know the path is set. Even if I could save her, she wouldn't want me to. This is her asking the universe for forgiveness. This is her paying reparations. I know her melter will chime that it's recharged, and it does. I know that she'll raise it to point at the king, and she does. I know that with that threat, she will draw the fire of every guard in the room, all at once, consuming her in a rain of plasma.

And she does.

The blasts hit her in several spots, but none of them kills her instantly. This is not a merciful way to die. It eats through her. The slow fire spreads until she disappears, and leaves nothing but a pile of dust. It accumulates where she stood, drifting on the air currents to form a swirling mound. Dee's screams pound and reverberate across the small hallway, until her lungs and vocal cords are melted in the same instant. The sudden end of the scream pulls me back to reality. It snaps me into a moment frozen in time where I'm given the chance to change things. *Dee took all their shots, and now they're disarmed. She knew this would give me a chance.*

Then, I realize I already started moving when the melter shots went off. My body made the decision while my brain processed Dee's death. My plasma sword is held out to my side as I close the gap to the nearest guard. It's an extension of my arm, of my will, here to execute my terrible, righteous rage. To my right, I catch a silvery flash and know Sophia is rushing the guards on that side. We are wrath. We are death. We are cosmic fucking justice, and we will make them all pay.

My sword sweeps upwards in a flash of blue, bisecting the nearest guard as he tries to hurriedly grab his sonic cannon. I flow through him into the next, sweeping his head from his shoulders with a horizontal slash. The third raises his cannon, but before he can squeeze off a shot, I spear him and the cannon with a final lunge, and then I rip the sword upwards and through him. The hallways is an echo of screams, a resonating orchestra that Sophia and I add fresh players to with every moment. I look to my right, and see the bloodbath left in Sophia's wake.

In the middle of the hallway, on the floor, is a man in a now scarlet red stained robe, crawling backwards and mumbling incoherently. He keeps trying to stand, but his legs seem to have failed him. Blood spray from his guards covers him, it drips from his arms and face, and mats down his hair. In all the realities he saw, none of them included us dispatching his guards so easily. So efficiently. Sophia grabs his shoulders from behind, and hauls him to his feet.

"But, but, how could you? This wasn't supposed to happen. The Narrator told me you would make us immortal, he told me—" he stammers, but shuts up when I put my plasma sword underneath his chin.

"Oh, I'll immortalize you, but you missed the point. The Narrator weaves us into stories. You assumed you're the main character, but you're not. You're a side-story, a secondary plot. Revealing, but ultimately, unimportant. You're just a sick, old man that loves abusing others. And I am so *fucking* tired of people like you!"

Before he can reply, I shove my sword through his neck. His eyes bulge, a scream crystallizing in them as I sever and cauterize his windpipe. Like a fish out of water, he tries to draw in breath, but my sword has sealed both sides of his throat. I watch with disgust as his mouth heaves in terrible shapes, alternating between trying to scream, and trying to supply oxygen to his failing body. I don't enjoy watching him suffer, but I do enjoy the knowledge that his death is painful, full of fear, and prolonged. It will take him agonizing minutes to die. As it should, it's what he's earned.

Sophia holds out the king's arm, and I sever his hand at the wrist. She drops his body on the floor, where it finishes the twitching and writhing of a fading life. We leave it behind, rush to the end of the hallway, and place his hand on the access panel to the underground facility. Before we step inside, I take one last look back, and say a silent thanks to Dee for her sacrifice.

We find the underground facility devoid of life, but unlike the hallway above, it's sterile and clean. As I walk the aisles, I see Dee's face in the twisted reflection from the gleaming metal surfaces. I'm surprised to see it's crying, tears streaming from its eyes, even though I can feel the moisture on my own cheek. I wander through the facility aimlessly, and Sophia follows. *These machines are the heart of it all, inhuman, uncaring. They turn suffering into a substance that feeds the cycle. This facility makes all the horror in this world possible. Here, injustice is propagated. These are the mechanisms of oppressors.*

My wandering has brought me in front of the giant, clear vat of Indigo. Of course it did. It churns slowly, uncaring, unshaken by the violence of the night. I stare into the blue, faintly glowing depths, and feel that familiar anger building inside me. There are decades of slavery that went into it, and to fuel what? An endless cycle of debauchery for a few rich people? A gleaming white marble palace? Some fool's vision to build a monarchy? *It's all such a fucking waste; short-sighted, pleasure-seeking bull-shit.* I realize my grip has tightened on the hilt of the plasma sword in my hand. I know why I wandered over to this tank. I know what I wanted to do.

I extend the sword and with one slash set the priceless fluid loose. It streams from the tank, soaking our feet, and swirls down through the drains on the floor. I look at Sophia and she nods in approval. We watch it all flow down until there's nothing left. And as the dregs disappear, I turn my fury on the processing equipment. I work down the aisles, methodically cutting each machine into a pile of scrap metal that oozes smoke and leaks oil. Wrath flows through my fingers, finding its birth in action, until the whole room is full of wreckage.

We find the mine cart in the corner of the facility. It's a simple mechanism to operate. A single, red button returns the cart to the mines. After we both position ourselves in the metal bucket, Sophia reaches out one long arm, and presses it. As we move down the tracks, I watch the receding opening to the facility until the direction curves, and it's obscured from sight.

In the near total darkness of the tunnels, I tell Sophia my story. Dee's death weighs on me, even though I knew her only momentarily. She was like me, I felt it. And now it's another debt I can't pay. Sporadic lights wash over us as we race down the mine track, marking our progress, and in their brief illumination I stare into her blank face and hope she understands. I've never told anyone this story before.

"My governess Sophia, the one I mentioned earlier and named you after, was with us for several years. She and I grew very close. I was a young girl in need of a mother, and even though she was only slightly older than me, she helped fill that void. She was a friend, a mentor, and a caretaker. I have so many fond memories from those years, when we'd curl up in the sunlight and she'd read to me.

"I got very sick. It grew in me slowly, but imagining myself like my mother, I didn't tell anyone. I hid my symptoms, and for a time no one noticed. And then they became impossible to hide. When my father found out, he was furious. The diagnosis was the same as my mother's. Cancer has spread through my young body, and it was eating me from the inside. There's some betrayal that's hidden in our genes, a terrible inheritance.

"There was a pride I felt from being strong like her. But my father wouldn't lose another person to something he could stop. He'd already planned against it. In Sophia's contract, if anyone in the family became terminally ill, she was required to take over the disease. This was standard practice in our city, all hired staff agreed to similar terms. I fought my father with all the strength I had left. I wanted to be free to make my own decisions, and I didn't want to take Sophia's future from her. Eventually, he had me sedated, and the operation was carried out while I was comatose."

I'm crying now, reliving the pain from it. Tears slide down my cheeks freely.

"So instead of being able to choose to die like my mother, I was cured at the expense of someone I loved. The loss broke me. I knew that I caused the pain she felt. I stayed at Sophia's bedside as she faded from the disease, and I apologized over and over. She would look into my eyes, cup my cheek, and smile. "*I would have gladly chosen to save your life anyways,*" she'd say."

Sophia reaches out in the dark, and lays her cool metal hand on my knee. It breaks my sobs free.

"You did not force her to do that, it is not your fault. You cannot blame yourself for how your city operated. Besides, you are worth sacrificing for. I see that, the Dorothy from this world saw it, and it sounds like your Sophia did as well. You are trying to change things, you are trying to make these worlds better. You are a good person," she says.

"I'm not worth that! Back in our city, I did awful things to tear down the disease transfer system. I killed hundreds of people, and at the time I swore that they deserved it. I did it for her, but I think now it would have broken her to see it. I wanted a world that wouldn't sacrifice some people to keep others alive, but I got there by using the same methods." The words tear out of me like flowing water from a tap that I can't shut. After I say them, the cold realization that it's the same thing Nick said to me is like a slap across my cheek.

"Sometimes, we take the only path we can see, and then later we realize it was not the right one. Even if it still took you where you were trying to go. You will have to forgive yourself for that, and learn from it."

I close my eyes, and see the scenes of death replay through my mind. The terror at the Skyball when deadly gas that I made was unleashed. The screaming. Crimson blood covering everything. My father on the floor of our home with a stump of an arm. My plasma sword held to Nick's throat, forcing him to sacrifice himself. Something in me shifts, and then breaks entirely. It shatters. A wall comes down, and great heaving sobs tear out of me. *I'm so sorry for it all, you were right Nick. I'm so fucking sorry.* Sophia wraps an arm around my shoulders, and I curl against her metal frame as our cart speeds into the dark.

FOURTEEN

NICHOLAS

For a moment, or maybe it's an eternity, we're frozen in time. From behind the guards bodies, my eyes lock with Dotty's as she stands on the lift. A warmth fills me. In that instant, I know I love her, and even more for the mistakes that she's made, for the flaws that make her human. And despite the distance, I see the same thing reflected in her face. That joy at seeing the only other person that's meaningful to you makes her eyes sparkle, as I'm certain mine do, and the corners of her lips twist up in a smile. It's only as an afterthought that I notice she's standing next to a giant automaton, and they're both covered in blood.

In the sunlight that floods the pit mine, the guard's black armor gleams. The robot next to Dotty glimmers in it, too. Food smells waft across the valley from the cornucopia on display on their ship. Near the well, another guard relaxes with the Allen of this world, drinking from a canteen. From the safety of their cave houses, the miners watch us all. There is a moment where it seems idyllic. For the barest of moments, there's peace.

When the guards reach to their hips for the melters, that peace is broken. *The lift is too far, they'll gun her down before she can get to cover. I've found her again, only to watch as she disappears. They'll turn her to dust and ruin the one thing that's left for me to love.* Anger soars through me, consuming everything in its blaze. *If she dies, I die.* And in that realization, I become their reckoning. My want to avoid violence sheds from me like chains that I've simply decided to not let bind me anymore. I spring the plasma knife from my wrist, and lunge for the nearest guard. A primal roar rips across the valley, shattering the silence. I realize only by the aftertaste that it came from me.

My knife splits through the back of the helmet of the nearest guard. He slumps under the weight of my charge, and we crash to the ground together. I turn in time to see the other raise his melter. Sunlight shines off the metal of the barrel. I pull my knife free, but I'm tangled with the first guard and can't get back to my feet quickly. *I'm too slow. I'm too fucking slow and Dotty will die for it.* I stare up in horror as he takes aim, and pulls the trigger.

A black blur hits the guard from the side just as he does, and it sends his shot careening into the wall of the cliff. The miners scream, but I ignore them. The black thing is on top of the guard, scratching with feral violence. It tears at his uniform and armor, but the claws don't penetrate, and the guard kicks the thing from him.

Charon hits the dirt in front of me, and I see then what the time in the wilderness has taken from him. He's thinner, his belly is starting to suck up into his spine. I can easily count his ribs now. It's only the starting phases of starvation, but it's clearly enough to rob his strength. He lies on the ground where the guard threw him, panting and exhausted. It breaks my heart seeing my friend like this.

I scramble to my feet just as the guard gains his. He pulls a plasma blade from his belt, and I position myself protectively in front of Charon. My plasma knife won't be worth much here, it's too short to get past his guard and too awkward to block a blow, but it's all I have and I'll die before they hurt him. The man in black armor raises his blade and pushes back on his outside heel. It's a stance that communicates instantly what I need to know—he's a competent swordsman, he's confident, and I'm fucked.

A mass of shimmering silver blasts through his chest, and showers me in blood. He grunts, looks down at the angular protrusion, gives one final jerk, and then stops moving. The thing is pointed like a spear, but too broad. It retracts, and the massive frame of the automaton stands up from behind the guard. Its blank face reflects my own back to me. I stare into its fathoms.

Dotty breaks the silence when she screams.

FIFTEEN

DOROTHY

A lift carries us from the glowing unreality of the mine. The underground cavern, receding now under our feet, was eerie and silent. Each passageway stood like a silent testament to the years that had been carved away here. And everywhere we looked were giant rocks that shimmered with that same iridescent blue as the vat of Indigo. Above our heads now sunlight fills the top of this shaft. I yearn for the freedom it promises.

When we crest the edge of land though, and break into the sunlight, it becomes immediately clear that something is wrong. On the hillside to our left, two guards stand in glistening black armor, appraising us. Further off to our right, Prince Allen and another guard are drinking from canteens and leaning against a well. The prince stares at me, dumbfounded.

Then I catch sight of Nick, and my heart leaps into my throat. He stands behind the two guards grinning at me. His face is covered in blood, and the comedy of him smiling despite all that forces me to smile in return. I realize how badly I've missed him in that moment, how long I've wanted to be back with him.

The arms of the guards near him jerk for their melters first, and my brain goes into a panic. *There's no way I can get there in time, nowhere to hide.* In a flash of silver, Sophia bolts towards them. Then, Nick's knife exits the front of one of their helmets.

From the corner of my eye, I see the guard near the well trying to unlatch the melter from his hip. There's something wrong with him though. His legs are shaking, unsteady, and his hands keep fumbling with the thing. Next to him, the prince looks barely able to stand. He leans heavily against the well for support. *Are they drugged? What the hell is happening here?* I rush for them, drawing my plasma sword.

A shot from a melter pierces the air behind me and careens into the cliff wall. A large chunk of it evaporates and sets a landslide of boulders free. Far behind me, I hear several others screaming, but I don't turn to look at them. I look back at the guards near Nick as I run, and see one of them pinned underneath a black animal that's a blur of claws. *Charon!*

I refocus on the guard near the well and see he's finally drawn his melter, and is steadying it toward Nick. The barrel dances around, unsteady as its wielder. I know in that instant that I won't close the distance in time.

"Get down!" I scream. I turn in time to see Nick and Sophia drop to the ground as the shot burns through the air where they just stood. It strikes the cliff face behind them, unleashing another torrent of boulders.

I turn back to see I've gained the guard's attention, and I keep charging. He drops the melter, the shot's wasted and now it has to recharge, and paws at the plasma blade on his hip. I grin as he nearly drops it in his hurried panic. He gets the blade out and spreads his legs wider to steady himself, but I'm already on him.

He raises his sword to chop down on me diagonally, but his timing is off. His entire movement pattern is slowed, and with his guard raised it leaves a perfect opening. I slash horizontally, my plasma sword a blur of speed, an extension of my arm. It cleaves him in two just above the waist. Dark arterial blood sprays onto grass that rustles serenely in the morning sun.

My momentum carries me slightly past the well, and when I whirl back around I see the prince supporting himself against the stone circle. Cradled in his lap is another melter that matches the gold of his armor. He steadies it in the crook of his thigh. It shines fiercely as it points towards me. *Fuck.*

"You...bitch," he mutters. From here, I can see his eyes won't hold steady. He keeps blinking as if trying to clear them, trying to keep them focused. They snap to me, and then wander away again. I stare at the barrel, afraid to move, afraid to breathe. There's nothing I can do. The point of the melter wavers, points back at me, and then his eyes focus over my shoulder. The melter jerks, and I feel the hot bolt of plasma arc near my shoulder and explode behind me. The prince slumps down against the cistern, and I spin around.

At first, there is only a cloud of pages. I'm transfixed watching as they float calmly into the sky. Lofted on invisible currents, their edges burning, sunlight races across them as they turn to dust, their words never to be read again. Sophia stands at the center of the maelstrom, her hands gripped to her chest where a gaping hole has formed. From between her metal fingers slips a steady stream of burning paper. Her blank metal gaze is fixed to the heavens, watching her books dissolve into nothing. Then she collapses.

Sixteen

Nicholas

The automaton was quicker. When the prince raised his melter, we both raced to Dotty's side. A mad dash in the hope that we might save her. The shot rang across the docile morning, and the world erupted into burning pages.

Dotty rushed to its side, and I rushed to hers. Smoke billowed from a charred hole in its central cavity. Choking back sobs, Dotty wrenched the door open and the remaining mass of burning paper and ash shot into the morning sky like so many doves. The interior chamber was a wreck of burn marks and exposed wiring. I wrapped my arms around Dotty as her sobs amplified.

Then, its hand moves. Dotty sees it and grabs it from the grass.

"Sophia! Sophia are you in there?!"

Sophia? It has a name?

The machine pushes itself up in the grass, smoke still streaming from the exposed cavity.

"It seems that my books absorbed the blast from the melter. It will take me some time to run a full diagnostic, but I appear, okay."

Dotty sobs again, and freeing herself from me, hugs the machine.

"I thought I had lost you too. I saw the pages, I thought you were gone. Like Dee, like Sophia, like my mom. I can't lose you."

I stand there speechless, unsure of what Dotty means. Then she turns back to me.

"Nick, this is Sophia, there's no reason to be scared of her. She's a friend I made from another world."

She?

Sophia inclines her head to me in greeting. "Nick, I have heard much about you. I am pleased to make your acquaintance."

"You saved me and Charon, I thought we were done for. Thank you," I say, and then remember Charon's emaciated form. I turn and find him limping towards us slowly. I walk over to him and bend down on my knee to hug him. He's still panting hard, obviously exhausted.

"I'm so sorry, boy. I knew you weren't getting enough food but I didn't know it was this bad."

He nuzzles his face against mine, too tired to respond, and I scratch him behind the ears. I grab him around all four legs and lift him up into my arms. I carry him onto the ship, so graciously left by the guards, set him in the shade of a parasol, and bring him a heaping plate of food from the table. He eats slowly, and then falls asleep with a deep, gratified purr coming from his chest.

When I turn back, Dotty is staring at me from Sophia's side.

There is a moment when I remember the enormity of the gulf between us. The betrayal and monumental devastation she caused, the way I lied to her and used her. It feels faded though, like an important thing from another time. Like it's only a curiosity now. The feeling of almost watching her die here is immediate and pressing. I love her, I knew it as soon as I saw her again, and I won't let another moment pass without honoring that.

We run into each other's embrace, and cling there like it's the only thing that keeps us safe. Her shape still feels familiar against mine. A missing piece that fits in place perfectly. We hold each other with all the ferocity and passion of people who have just nearly died, and cry. Great, heaving sobs break free from her, and they unleash the same thing in me.

"I'm so sorry Nick, for everything. I've done terrible things, it's so clear to me now," she gets out between sobs.

My heart soars. *There can be forgiveness here.* I hold the back of her head as it rests against my chest and gently stroke her hair. "It's okay. I know you needed to change things, I know you didn't see another way to do it. I'm sorry too, Dotty. I lied to you, I used you."

She raises her head and meets my gaze. Our tear streaked faces are both covered in blood. She reaches a hand up, and swipes her thumb across my lips. She pulls my face down to kiss her, and I close my eyes to savor every instant of it.

When we part, she smiles coyly at me and says, "That's the first kiss where I knew your real name."

"The first of many," I say, and kiss her again.

As reality returns, we both separate and look around the valley. Sophia sits on the ground, her hand stroking the grass. Faint trails of smoke still rise from her chest. Against the well lies Prince Allen, gleaming in his golden armor.

"What should we do with the prince?" Dotty asks.

"Let the miners decide, they have decades spent under his cruelty," I say. As I look around the clearing, they slowly start to drift out of their caves toward us. A few are bloody or injured from falling debris, but they all smile and wave to us triumphantly.

The next hours are a blur of commotion as we off-load the food from the ship, and load on anything the miners intend to travel with. There aren't many possessions left between them, but it's still chaos as they each try to secure their belongings. Brian and Henry use a hand severed from one of the guards to gain access to the pilot's cabin. Once they have the door open, they jam it using a spar of wood cut from the table. Dotty and I scan the sky intermittently, nervous that the palace will mount a response before we can take off.

At some point, the prince is bound, gagged, and hauled over to the lip of the shaft that connects to the mine. A group of miners stand there now, and more congregate as their work finishes. I can't hear the discussion from where I sit on the deck of the ship, but I can imagine the contents of it.

"Might have been a mercy for them if you'd done the deed yourself," says Brian to me, as he walks back onto the ship.

I raise an eyebrow to him. "Not going to help them decide, then?"

"Nah, I never had a heart for violence. Mind, I won't stop them neither. I know that man deserves what's coming."

We both turn back to watch the simmering crowd, as Dotty and Sophia, the hole in her front cavity the only lingering sign of her injury, march up the ramp to join us on the ship. The miners were nervous around the automaton at first, but as soon as she showed her impressive strength and willingness to help they warmed to her quickly. For her part, she seemed thrilled with meeting so many new people, and excitedly introduced herself to each of the miners. Dotty on the other hand has been more reticent and reclusive, especially after I introduced her to Brian and Josephine.

As we all stand watching, the crowd backs up several paces, leaving a lone figure on his knees at the edge of the shaft. His head is bowed against the rising sun. They've pulled his gold armor off, leaving him only in simple, white underclothes. There is no ceremony. No speech is given to mark the occasion. One of the miners simply walks forward, kicks him in the back, and the prince disappears over the edge. Faintly, I hear his muffled scream echo up out of the mine, and it sends a shiver down my spine.

I turn to Dotty and see a sour expression on her face. When I give her a curious glance, she shakes her head at me. Whatever it is, she doesn't want to discuss it now.

Their deed done, the miners slowly move back to the ship. Once all are loaded, Brian gives Josephine a signal. She wasn't sure about being our pilot, but I had a suspicion that she'd have a preternatural talent for it. As we gracefully lift into the air and arc towards the city, I know I was right to.

There's quiet on the ship as we watch the pit mine sink beneath our feet. I wonder how it must feel for the miners who have been trapped here for decades. I catch Brian's eyes full of tears, and reach out to squeeze his shoulder as the mine fades from view.

Shouts of fear and worry go up from the miners, and I turn around and follow their outstretched fingers. On the horizon, four flat shapes are now visible racing towards us from the direction of the palace. In the brief moment that I watch them grow larger, it's clear that they're closing the distance to us fast.

"Oh fuck! Dotty, we have company incoming." I find her face in the crowd, it's drawn in anger. She nods in response. "Everyone, brace yourselves against the railing! Joe, can we move any quicker?"

The miners all fan out to the railings, grabbing handholds and crouching closer to the ground. There's a small increase in thrust from the ship as Josephine pins it, but a quick check confirms that the shapes are still gaining on us. I can already make out the number of people aboard each craft — there's just a handful on each of them. No wonder they're moving faster, we're loaded down with thirty miners and their belongings.

In an instant, they're on us. The ships pull up alongside, on top, and behind us. On each of their decks are men and women in tuxedos and cocktail dresses that whip around in the wind. There are chefs, butlers, and scientists alongside them. They carry gleaming sonic cannons in their dainty, manicured hands. It's an image that would look ridiculous if it wasn't also full of danger.

Several things happen at once.

"Take them down!" The shouts go up from the other ships, and sonic cannons are leveled at us.

"Incoming!" I shout, and crouch down with an iron grip on the railing.

"Evasive maneuvers!" shouts Josephine from the cabin.

We plummet from the sky. A torrent of bursts from sonic cannons fills the void that we left behind. Around me, miners hold tight onto the railing as their belongings and the table of food are left somewhere in the space we used to inhabit. On the other side of the ship, Sophia has one arm wrapped around Charon and the other grips the railing. *Bless that robot.* Behind us, two of the other ships race to follow our path.

The canopy of trees rushes towards us, all purples and reds in the rising afternoon sun. The smell of warm sap drifts above them as we close the distance. *We're going too fast, Josephine won't be able to pull this off. She needs to pull up. Oh fuck, fuck—*

"Hold on everyone!" Josephine shouts from the pilot's cabin.

The ships arcs, and gravity reverses. I'm slammed into the deck of the ship by the force of it. Through my face the whine of the engines and the creaking of the metal hull form a symphony of noise. There's no way it was built with acrobatics like this in mind. *Just hold dammit, just hold.* The pressure eases, and we rocket back into the sky. My arm, wrapped around the railing still, snaps taught as we enter a nearly vertical ascent, and I look behind us.

There's a mass of broken trees where one ship didn't pull up in time. Around me, miners grip tight to the railings, the strength they've built through decades of hard labor on display. The other craft follows us still, but as I watch, men and women are jettisoned from over its railing like so much useless cargo. They fly off the edge in a tumult of cocktail dresses and flapping tuxedo tails when their meager muscles give out. Likely noticing the same thing, the vessel suddenly levels out and stops their pursuit.

We stop our ascent soon after. On the horizon, the city is much closer now. One of the other pursuing ships appears above our deck, and from it two guards drop. They land on our deck with force, causing the ship to dip slightly, and draw their melters and plasma swords.

"Turn this damn thing around or we start finding out how many of you rats we can kill!" one of them shouts over the rushing wind.

I look to the city to judge how close we are. The surface of it is like a moving mosaic, like a living sea of metallic tiles float and froth there. *What the hell is that?*

"We're not stopping anything," Brian says, and I flip back around.

He's left the pilot's cabin, and is standing in front of the two guards with a plasma pick in hand. *He must have stolen one from the mines.* I stand up, my shoulder aching from the stress of holding the railing, and join him. From the other side of the ship, Dotty and Sophia do the same. The miners form a circle around the guards, their eyes hungry and full of hate.

The guards, realizing that they are far outnumbered, spin around. They swing their melters wildly at the crowd.

"Stay back, stay back damn you! If you don't stay back we'll fucking melt you!"

In the onrush of wind, we are all still. The moment before violence hangs, poised like a guillotine blade, waiting for that first movement. And in that void, a buzzing fills the air. It starts at the back of my head, but as it gets louder it breaks through our tension, and I notice miners starting to look around.

"The city's defenses are activated, grab onto the railing!" Josephine shouts from the pilot's cabin.

I whirl around. The city is covered in a seething mass of Inquisitors. They move like so many ants, crawling over each other. I remember nearly being overrun by their swarm in our city. Then, the pattern breaks. At once, the Inquisitors all take flight, and darken the sky around the city. They race towards us like a thundercloud.

"The railing, now!" shouts Josephine again, breaking us all from our stupor.

I run to the railing and throw my arm around it again, just as the dam breaks. The guards stand in the center of our ship, dumbfounded. A rain of Inquisitors falls towards them, and they fire their melters into it, screaming into the flow of metal. With a great shattering, they are sheared from existence. The tide of machines punches a great hole in our ship, right through where the guards stood, and it lurches and tumbles.

We are so many leaves in the wind. I hold onto the railing as we spin and roll out of control. My shoulder screams in pain, but I hold as I'm repeatedly slammed into the railing and those around me. Inside the pilot's cabin, Josephine wrestles with the controls to the ship. She's strapped into a chair, the only fixed object on our ship.

Through the shifting images, I see the canopy of trees getting closer. It's our death, the tide that will swallow us. Above us, a writhing mass of Inquisitors has torn the remaining ships, and people on them, to shreds. They explode, but no sound reaches me past the rush of wind and pounding of blood in my ears.

"Fuck!" Josephine screams, and then with one great lurch the ship corrects and stabilizes, as if righted by an invisible hand.

We rocket into the open door of the city, and grind to a halt across its promenade. Debris flies everywhere. Bits of plant and stone from the walk cascade over the prow of the ship to land behind us. When we finally halt, miraculously okay, I stand and watch the great mass of Inquisitors crawl back into their nests on the exterior of the city. Behind us is an avenue of destruction, and in the trees at the entrance to the city burns the wreckage of two other ships.

Our reception in the city is magnificent. As we unload from the wrecked ship, a crowd slowly gathers, flying down from all parts of the city as the word spreads. A trickle at first, and then a torrent. They stay clear of the miners. There is a nervous tension growing on both sides with each passing second, and then the dam breaks.

"Brian?!" Someone cries out from the gathering crowd. I turn to look as an older, graying woman pushes her way through to the front, and hear a choked sob break loose from Brian. He runs to her, and they embrace.

The scene plays out again, and again as the miners are recognized by their surviving families, friends, and old lovers. Cheers erupt around us, and tears of joy and happiness flow freely. It infects us too, and when I see Dotty crying at the moment, I pull her close again. It's a reunion for us all.

Jasmine steps forward from the crowd, a grin splitting her face. She puts her hands together, and bows deeply to me. There's a solemn thankfulness to it, and I respond with the same gesture.

"I thought you were dead, or lost forever to the mines! Surely didn't expect to see you again. I see you found your boo too, and freed the miners while you were at it." She juts her hand out to Dotty, who shakes it. "I'm Jasmine. We saw you when you came through, but ignored you on account of your robot."

"That's Sophia, and I'm Dorothy. She's nothing to be concerned about."

"She?" Jasmine asks, her eyebrows raised.

"Yes, Dorothy is kind enough to identify me as a person and not a thing. Although I am still unsure if the gendered term fits well. Jasmine, what are those small humans over there?"

"The children?"

"Children? Hmm, I have never seen anything like them. They are quite energetic."

Stirred on by the energy in the room, the young ones run and jump at the fringes of the crowd. They collide with themselves and others in their enthusiasm, which only makes them run faster and jump higher.

Jasmine laughs deeply. "Come with me, Sophia, I'll introduce you. I think they're going to *love* you." With that she grabs Sophia's arm and steers her back towards the crowd. As they walk away, she calls over her shoulder, "we'll be having a feast tonight to celebrate, best get some rest before then!"

The three of us watch Sophia disappear into the crowd. We hear peels of laughter as the children meet her, and immediately start to climb her towering frame. It's the sweetest homecoming I can imagine, but it doesn't feel like ours.

"I know a pretty good park near here we can rest in," I say, turning to Dotty with a smile.

She smiles back, tiredness etching her face. "That sounds lovely."

Under the shade of trees, we lay on lush grass and tell each other the details of our separate journeys. I'm shocked to hear about the origin of Sophia, and her brush with the Narrator when she entered the city.

"We've got to stop him, all of these worlds are just his plaything. He's manipulating all of us," I say, when she stops talking for a time.

She nods, propped up against a tree and staring out into the city. "What do you think he wants? It doesn't seem just *malicious* to me. If he wanted to just kill us all, I'm assuming he probably could."

"I think it's like he told me, back before we left our city. He wants to create a good story. We're just characters in a play for his enjoyment." There's a thought forming about what he really wants, but I can't put it into words yet. *He wants to experience something definitively new, but what exactly?*

"Nick, could you see the lines, or pathways or whatever, out there? You know, in the Cosmos?"

I look up into her eyes and nod. "Ever since we left our city I could see them. I think he did something to me, he said something about giving me the vision to see the map."

"And you can't deviate from it, even if you try?"

"That's right, it seems to be always where I am, like I was always going to go there."

"Sophia said it might be something that protects us since we're '*three-dimensional beings in a four-dimensional space*', but I had no clue what she meant. Do you think the Narrator controls them?"

"I've been thinking about that too. If he doesn't, something or someone must. What do you think the chances are that we'd wind up heading to the same city otherwise?"

"Right, that's what I thought too. So it doesn't really matter if we want to stop him or not, it might not be up to us at all."

"That was the same conclusion I came to. I feel completely powerless when I think about it like that. But I still *feel* like I'm the one in control. I don't feel like someone else is making decisions for me. I could still decide to do nothing at all, right? Maybe the Narrator just supplies guidance, like he gave you when you came into the city? Maybe that's all he can do."

She nods at that, and we're both lost in thought for some time. At my feet, Charon wakes, stretches mightily, finds a comfortable position leaning against Dotty after circling twice, and falls back asleep. As we watch, the miners filter off through the city with their families and friends. They've returned home at last. It reminds me how far we've come from ours, and yet again my thoughts are drawn back to our city.

"When the prince had me down in their facility, he told me that if they stopped taking Indigo they might start aging rapidly. Nick, listen. I'm worried that the miners will all die soon. I destroyed all the remaining Indigo. I destroyed all the machinery that made it. I destroyed it all, and I didn't think twice about the effect it would have. It just seemed like there couldn't be justice as long as it existed. I'm learning that pursuing what's just isn't always compassionate." The words are a torrent, they rush from her. She looks back at me, silent tears streaking her face now, and I understand what I saw eating at her earlier.

I stare into her eyes, and I understand. It's the same reason that she sacrificed people to change things in our city. She wants justice, no matter the cost. I want to eliminate suffering, and couldn't give a damn for what's just. But if she hadn't destroyed their Indigo supply, surely another would take control from the Castle, and nothing would have changed. She may have sacrificed the miners, but she's saved this whole damn planet from more years of oppression.

"We can tell Brian. You made a hard choice, and I'm sure it will have consequences—"

"But I *knew*. I knew what it could do, and I still destroyed it. There's this anger inside me. All I could feel was an overwhelming rage, and the need to tear it all down."

"And if you hadn't, someone would have recreated what the king had built. Do you think those miners would have wanted their freedom so they could watch the city's children get funneled into the same life later on? Maybe there's not always a clean way out. Sometimes, someone has to get hurt, even if they don't deserve it. If it had been me down there, I might not have made the same call, but then these people would pay for it for generations. You broke the cycle."

"Nick, am I a monster?"

I move to sit next to her, and wrap my arm around her. "We've both done monstrous things, but I don't think we're monsters."

She leans her head against my shoulder, and sobs. They're great, heaving things, and I comfort her until she stills. The tension in her shoulders dissipates, and she finally relaxes. We watch the lazy afternoon sun drift across the city.

A rhythmic thumping builds slowly, until it consumes every other sound around it. Conversations die in its wake, as more fists and metal cups are slammed against the table to amplify the beat. It builds until it throbs in my psyche. And then, with impeccable coordination, everyone stops simultaneously. There is total silence.

A man stands at the head of our long, wooden table, and I realize he looks strikingly similar to Jasmine. His hair is shoulder length and starkly white, but his frame is muscular and healthy. "Friends, old and new, welcome. Tonight we celebrate the return of our people from the mines, something that this old man never thought he'd see. They were put into bondage decades ago, and forced to work hard every day since. My friends, you were slaves, but now you are once again free. Welcome to The People." A cheer erupts from the crowd at this, but the man holds up his hands for silence. "They were freed by four travelers, who none of us knew or asked for help. They saw something broken with our world, and they fixed it. My friends, you were travelers, but now you are once again home. Welcome to The People."

The cheer from this is deafening. It echoes across the city and bleeds out into the night around us. I look up, and imagine that the moons might hear it in the sky. Suddenly, the aisles between the tables are filled with people. An arm reaches over, and my cup is filled with something bubbly. Plates of food are passed out after that. They're full of fresh vegetables from the garden and the smell is magnificent. I wink at Dotty across the table, and tip my glass to her. She smiles wholeheartedly in return.

There's a cascade of children's laughter, and I look around to see Sophia walking toward our table. She's holding a child in each arm, has one sat on her shoulders, and another two hold onto her legs as she walks. Her chest cavity has been opened and scrubbed clean, and what was once a sanctum to words and ideas is now a cubby hole for a gap-toothed, grinning toddler. The glow from the table light hits her, and I see that they've colored a ridiculous toothy-smile and squinting eyes on her otherwise blank face. Dotty and I can't contain our laughter at the sight.

"Sophia, your face!" Dotty gets out between laughs.

"I know. I told the children they may draw on me as long as it was appropriate. Besides, I have never had a face before."

Dotty and I are struck dumb at this for a moment. *How strange it must be to be a thinking thing without a face to express emotion.* But the sight of it is still too funny, too separated from her sleek metal frame, and we start laughing again. In a great unloading, the children all scramble off of her and run through the room to find their families. Sophia moves over to take an open seat at the head of the table between us. She evaluates the chair with distrust for a moment, and then moves it aside to sit cross-legged at the table.

"Sophia, what did you think about the children?" Dotty asks her, composing herself again.

"I think, I feel happy around them. They are so full of life." Sophia stares off after the children.

"I couldn't be happier for you," Dotty responds.

"Thank you, Dorothy. Without you, I would still be alone in that mausoleum. None of this would have been possible. What will you two do now? How will you find the Narrator?"

"I think it's time we try to have another chat with him, and see if he wants to offer more guidance," Dotty says, her eyes fixed on mine.

Seventeen

Dorothy

After our feast concludes, Nick and I head back to an apartment in Sun Gate that Jasmine coordinated for us. Our bellies are full, and our heads thick with the fruit wine that kept filling our cups. Even Charon looks to be starting to fill back in after his time starving in the jungle. He paws along behind us softly, swaying with sleep. Sophia finds a nearby charging pad, her body still covered in paint. Exhaustion has come for us all.

The apartment is a suite in one of the golden towers that adjoins the park we laid in earlier. The tower sways rhythmically, as do all the neighboring towers, gathering static electricity from the air as they do. Nick and Charon seem distrustful of the movement at first, but when we open the door it becomes clear to them that the inside remains stationary while only the external shell moves.

The swaying buildings have always seemed like a strange choice by the designers. They're both a sign, and generator of, excess energy for the city. When flying above them, they appear like golden grass swaying in the breeze. I always thought it was more of an aesthetic consideration than a practical one.

Our suite takes up the entire first floor, and the building is otherwise unoccupied. Like most doors in Sun Gate, the entrance is made from living metal. As we approach, the shimmering gold wall parts like a stage curtain and disappears. Behind it is a luxurious entertaining space that is dominated by two soft-looking purple sofas laid onto dark hardwood flooring. From here, I know the layout branches into bedrooms and bathrooms on the left, and a kitchen and study on the right. I've seen my share of the inside of these apartments from my time in Sun Gate.

Charon doesn't wait for an invitation, and plods over to one of the couches. He hops onto it, stretches his back deeply, and then lays down and closes his eyes. I grab Nick's hand and guide him back to the bathroom. It's our first time alone, but both of us are covered in filth. We were only able to wash off the worst of the blood before the feast in a public washroom.

There is a hunger growing in his eyes, and the same burns in the pit of my stomach. The bathroom is expansive and tiled. A glass-walled shower fills the room, the ceiling above it covered in multiple water heads. We both undress, and when Nick reaches for my waist, I slap his hand away playfully and waggle my finger. I turn and move into the shower, rocking my hips playfully. He follows behind with a smile on his lips.

The water pours over us in a soft, warm rain as soon as we enter. I find two sachets of soap and hand one to Nick. We clean each other, starting at the top, and with growing anticipation, moving slowly downwards. His touch teases my skin, filling our desire until it cascades over. When he leans in to kiss me, I take it in greedily. I reach down and grab him as we kiss, and feel his body respond instantly to the touch. The pressure in my stomach builds and builds until it must be satisfied.

My need is overwhelming. I pull him over to one of the glass walls and lean my arms against it. My breasts spread out against the glass, and I turn around to catch his hungry gaze as he grabs my hips from behind. We find the root of our desire together, panting and moaning into the night. Afterwards, when we're clean again, we leave the shower and find our bed without turning the lights on.

I wake in the early dark of morning and dress quietly. Nick is still fast asleep. I can hear it in his slow, steady breathing as he lays nearly face down on the massive expanse of bed. Last night, we both avoided the topic of *who* would have a discussion with the Narrator. There is only room for one in the human-shaped cavity at the top of the city. I don't intend to let it be a decision we make together. I know it needs to be me.

I walk softly back to the entrance to the suite, and when Charon's head raises slightly in the darkness, I move over and pet him.

"I'm going to try and talk with the Narrator, bring Nick to me if he wakes," I whisper. Charon nods his head slightly, and then slumps it back down on the couch.

I wind through the park outside in the darkness, one of several ghosts. This must be when most of the city does work on their fields and orchards. Before the weight of the oppressive sun blankets everything. They're all shadows flying silently in the pre-dawn light, and I drift amongst them towards the tower that dominates over it all.

The inner corridors and elevator are softly lit, but it feels like a violation after the cloak of darkness outside. I rise upwards. *Is the Narrator drawing us in, or playing us along? Surely he knows we want to destroy him. If he's not afraid, does that mean we're doomed to failure?* The elevator softly chimes at the top floor and wakes me from my thoughts.

I walk out into the grand hallway, open here to the outside world, and see it's bathed in the light of twin moons that sit low on the horizon. It illuminates the rows of plants in a soft yellow, and leaves stark shadows behind them. I close my eyes, and for a moment see an overlap of all the cities I've visited. Cities where this massive domed hallway was home to a monster, and others where it was a mausoleum. I open my eyes to find Jasmine walking towards me from the aisles. She's wearing overalls, gardening gloves that are smeared in dirt, and carries a small trowel in one hand.

"What're you doing up here so early?" she asks in a quiet voice. The darkness works on her too, and she doesn't want to break the spell by talking too loudly.

"There's a machine in the room beyond this. I need to use it to try and figure out where Nick and I should head next."

"What're you all trying to find?"

"An old man that's playing games with us."

"Was he the one that you fought with last time?"

Ah, so they were watching that.

"Yes, sort of. That was some kind of...apparition. A ghost. We need to find the real him."

She nods, perplexed. "How will the machine tell you all that?"

I clench my jaw, and try to not let my frustration show. *Please just get out of my way, girl.* "It's some sort of dimensional transport, it allows us to be ghosts and talk with the old man."

She pauses for a while, thinking. I'm tempted to walk past, but I don't want to offend her. My irritation is growing quickly though. Nick has so much more patience than I do. "So, this old man, is he trapped in the machine then?"

I'm about to tell her how ridiculous that sounds, and then I stop myself. *Is it ridiculous? He's not trapped in circuits and wires, but is he trapped in this other dimension?* "That's an interesting idea, Jasmine. You've given me something to consider. Would you like to come along and watch?"

She shrugs and nods, sets down her gloves and trowel, and follows me through the rows of plants. Their fragrance is muted in the cool night, not like when I walked through here under the sun's gaze. In the moonlight, dew reflects on their leaves and berries. It's like walking through a dark hallway lined with shimmering jewels. For a moment I'm caught by the beauty.

We walk from the grand hall, and through the adjoining clean room. Nothing springs outwards to hose us off. I remember when Nick and I discovered the purpose of this room after our battle with Cerberus, and smile at the memory. We both thought that it was another defense mechanism at first. On the other side, the control room is silent and dark. Moonlight streams in from the window, blanketing the room in a solid stripe of yellow light.

I navigate to the dimensional transit machine, and it moves silently open to greet me. There's a stain of dried blood on the edge that catches my eye. *Is that from when Nick met the Narrator earlier?* I turn back to Jasmine, I can see her eyes are wide in the darkness. "If anything goes wrong, get Nick." She nods in response. I take a deep breath, and step inside.

When I open my eyes, a white porcelain cup fills my vision. Steam rises from it, obscuring my vision. There's no smell connected to the red liquid inside. It has all of the physicality of a real thing, but without the sensation. I realize I'm holding the tea cup in my own hand, and move it away from my face. My surroundings come into focus.

I sit in a deeply cushioned, high-backed armchair, directly opposed by another of the same style. The deep maroon velvet was beautiful once, but is worn and missing buttons now. Between the two chairs is a small wooden table with another tea cup, just like mine, on it. I set mine next to it, and feel nothing.

Sitting opposite me is the Narrator. He's dressed in the same black tuxedo he always is. His legs are crossed and a perfect smile splits his old face.

"Well hullo, Dorothy. I thought we'd have a more civil meeting than our last *entanglement*. Although I must admit, I did love the framing of it. There's always so much drama with you!"

Anger roars through me, instantly flaring to life at his taunt. I want to tear this old man apart for everything he's done, for treating our lives like some game. I remind myself that I need to get information though, and swallow it. "Where are we?" I ask through gritted teeth.

"Now, that is an interesting question! So direct. So simple, yet full of menace. But I'm afraid it's the wrong question. We are, well, nowhere. Or everywhere, really. Or maybe it's most accurate to say that everywhere is contained here? It's at least not a frame of reference that is really understandable."

"What *is* the right question, then?" I ask, clenching my hand with no sensation, and barely restraining myself.

"*What* is the right question! You're absolutely right." He looks around himself, taking it all in. "What is this place? Tell me Dorothy, what do you think that space between cities was? Where does it exist?"

I open my mouth, and then close it again. *What is it, actually? I've taken it as a means to an end.* I think back on what Sophia said, '*a four-dimensional plane*' she called it. "A four-dimensional plane?"

The Narrator's eyes snap to mine, a grin splitting his face and a sudden fire in his eyes. He leans forward to the edge of his seat, his face spanning across the wooden table. "That robot was more clever than I gave her credit for. Yes, my dear, that's completely right. But a three-dimensional creature can't comprehend a four-dimensional space, so we created a way to guide you through it."

We? "The tunnels?" *A 'probability density function' Sophia called them.*

"Ding ding ding, right again!" The Narrator rockets out of his seat and jumps to his feet, so much faster than an old man should be capable of. "Come with me, Dorothy. I want you to see something."

I rise, and hesitantly follow him to a bank of screens. It's an enormous, towering stretch that curves around at either end, where some of the displays have fallen from the pile and lie smashed on the ground. The Narrator snaps his fingers, and different scenes show up on each one in front of me. It's overwhelming at first, so I focus on one at a time.

My eyes are first drawn to one that shows Cerberus, that freakish monstrosity that guarded the control room of our city. There's something bloody in his hands, and when I lean closer I see that it's two halves of a human body clad all in black. With a shiver, I realize it's my own. There's an unrealness in seeing your own corpse, an impossibility, and it makes me woozy with vertigo.

"You have to understand, I've seen this story play out in so many different ways. An infinite number of ways really, and it just wasn't satisfactory. No one wants to tell a story where the hero dies immediately."

His words barely register. The next screen shows Nick vomiting blood, and succumbing to the poison I used at the Skyball.

"Every twist, every turn. I guided you both."

I rush through the screens, taking them in as quickly as I can. Another shows the burning wreckage of our flier, crashed into the treetops of this alien world.

"I couldn't let you both be lost."

There's me in a bloody heap, mauled by Charon after I betrayed Nick.

"Or pointlessly wasted."

This one shows Nick and Charon, their lifeless bodies thrown on a raging fire in the middle of a burnt out city.

"And the ending is just as important as what comes in between. It had to be the right ending."

And here I am, dressed all in marble white. Pregnant, and holding another child in my arms. The arm of Prince Allen slung over my shoulder, and a defeated scowl on my face.

I whirl on him. "But why interfere with us at all? Why play these games with our worlds? You have the power to make things better, and you choose to watch us suffer. You deliberately sabotage an entire city to see if you can make a robot become sentient. You enslave a population for decades to have Nick and I free them. It's insane!"

"But darling, without me to help you build the plot, think of how boring it would all be! There'd be no grand arcs, no pacing, no recognizable character development—"

"We're not your fucking characters!" I scream, and lunge for him. My body passes right through his, like I'm a ghost, or a shadow. I spin back around, a growl building inside me, and notice the world is fading.

"Come convince me! It ends where it began, Dorothy," the Narrator says, and bows as around us everything fades away into blackness.

I blink, and I see the lid of the dimensional transit machine again. It springs open, and I'm greeted by stares from Nick, Jasmine, Sophia, and Charon. They heave a collective sigh of relief.

Eighteen

Nicholas

"It ends where it began," I repeat, after Dorothy finishes recounting her meeting with the Narrator. My eyes meet hers, and there's a recognition of our shared past. Our shared motivations. Our origin story.

"The Box," we both say at the same time.

"But what's all this with dimensional planes?" I ask.

"And what were all those different endings I saw?" she adds.

Charon paces the room, obviously stirred to discomfort from the conversation. Jasmine's eyes dart between us all, confusion etched on her face. *There's no time to fix that now.*

Sophia sighs, and all our eyes turn to her. Even Charon stops his pacing, and sits on his haunches attentively.

"I believe it is time to share the full history of the city with you. You have to understand, all Great Mothers and Fathers are born with this knowledge. As it was programmed by my creators, the same ones that built these cities, I do not know how truthful it is. It was considered that only cities which met certain criteria were ready for it. There were fears that if humanity's darker ambitions took hold in a city, with this knowledge we might see a new age of colonialism. From what I saw in the palace, I believe this assessment was well made. Jasmine, as a representative of this city, I expect that you will carry this to your people. From what I have seen, they are prepared for it.

"The cities were born out of a dire need. Humanity had poisoned their first planet, and knew their time as a species there was limited. Overpopulation, dwindling natural resources, and a cycle of drought and blight led to mass starvation. Climate change, and the mega storms it brought, caused the surface of the planet to be nearly unlivable. Creation of these seed ships, that would launch into various trajectories across the galaxy, stretched the remaining resources to the breaking point. It was the last gambit of a dying civilization.

"There were numerous technical challenges. Chief amongst them was population control. Simulations showed that using the wrong method to control the population density could easily result in societal collapse. Not only was it necessary to control the number of people, but also to maintain some form of societal hierarchy. It was generally understood that this brought order to the system, even as it removed equality. There was a tipping point when revolution would occur, but up to this point, a caste-type system improved stability.

"Secondarily, there was a desire to maintain some physical connection between the cities. Although some argued this was unnecessary, it was the hope of many of the creators that our cities would knit together and create a connected civilization even as we blew apart like dust through the galaxy. Interstellar transit technology available at the time would not have made this feasible, it was far too slow, so a team began to research inter-dimensional transit.

"Solutions to both problems were discovered by the same team. As they developed an understanding of higher dimensions, they found that not only could we travel through a fourth dimensional space inside of a timeline to remove great distances, but that if we looked even higher to a fifth dimensional space, we could understand the potentialities of all the different, infinite timelines. They also found that certain qualities could be transferred across these timelines, and from this knowledge, the Box was created.

"You already know that the cities are connected through a fourth dimensional space. It allows transit across unimaginable distances. The Box uses a similar technology to transfer disease across timelines, either between two participants, or between two versions of yourself. Describing the Box as *curing disease* is not quite correct then. In reality, it just packages a quality about you, and moves it to somewhere else. You know the outcomes from here. It allowed your cities to survive, even as it created generational oppression.

"What has become clear to me now is that there must have been a third outcome of this discovery. One that we were not programmed with knowledge of. To transit a fourth dimensional plane, a guide is necessary. Even when it is not visible to the user, it keeps them locked in their timeline, constrained to a determinate path. I was not aware of this until we stepped into the Cosmos. This would require an entity that operated at a higher level to construct. And if the fifth dimension was accessible, if the possibilities of all the timelines could be understood, the creators would want someone, or something, to steer our future away from disaster. I think this is why Dorothy saw all those different potential endings for you both."

"So you're saying that the Narrator could have been part of the creator's plan?" I ask.

"Maybe not as such, and maybe he did not always try to manipulate outcomes in the same way. But in some capacity, yes, I think that is likely."

"But how could he have survived this long?" Dotty asks.

Sophia shrugs in response. It's the most human expression I've ever seen her make and I smile at the sight of her towering metal body making the gesture. "When we were in the fourth dimensional Cosmos, I observed that time was stilled, or at least very slowed. I would imagine that the same holds true for the fifth dimension. Besides, we do not know what he is. He appears human, but could be something else entirely."

"But he is real, right? When I've tried to interact with him, I just pass right through him."

I think back to the wall of glass I watched crash into him in the Skyball. How I was sure he was dead, only to see him later, unharmed. Then I remember the video Brian showed me, in a time that seems so long ago now, where an old man dragged me to a disease transfer machine and saved me from the cancer that was killing me.

"He must be. Before all of this started, before I became Allen, he dragged me from my hospital bed where I was dying from cancer, and saved me using the Box." '*It ends where it began*' echoes again in my head.

Dotty whirls on me. "You never told me that!"

Now it's my turn to shrug. "It just never seemed pertinent, just another one of his manipulations."

"So mostly he must visit our timeline as a projection, like a shadow from the fifth dimension that's cast down to our third dimension," Sophia adds, nodding.

"So if we can make it to where he resides, to this fifth dimension, we can hurt him there. We can put an end to all this." Dotty's staring down at the floor as she says it, but her face is etched in anger.

"Sophia, if the Box uses some fifth dimensional connection to transfer diseases, can we access this plane from it?" I ask.

"It seems sensible, and that aligns with what the Narrator said, but I do not know how this is done."

Dotty's face turns to mine, and in her eyes I see it all. I see her mother succumbing to cancer. I see her governess Sophia dying to save her. I see her greatest regret, the horror of the Skyball. I see the fresh anger at what happened to this Sophia's world, and at being imprisoned as a living womb.

And I feel it too. The death of my dad, the death of Brian. The weight of becoming someone else, just to try and change things. Encountering world after world torn apart by a madman. Our histories are intertwined with The Box and the Narrator. Like how a kaleidoscope rotates to create different images using only mirrors and the same base materials, we keep circling around them.

Finally, there is a possibility for something different, for an end. A way out. A way to smash the glass jar that holds us, and write our own story. We have to take it.

"Jasmine, can you take us to the nearest disease transfer machine?" I ask. She's been observing us in silence, listening and absorbing. Her eyes are questioning, but she nods.

"Of course."

Dotty and I prepare in silence. There's a fatal air that hangs over us, but also a determination. The approach of an end doesn't fill me with fear, surprisingly, but resolve. *If the Narrator knows all possibilities, then he can't lose. But still we have to try.*

From Jasmine, I acquire a plasma blade. She brings it with her along with steaming plates of food on a tray. I meet Dotty's eyes, and then Charon's, and see my thoughts reflected in both of theirs. *A final meal.* It's delicious of course, and packed with vegetables and fruit grown in the city. The meat is still generated from nutrient blocks, but Charon wolfs it down greedily. It's a final reminder of the life that they've built here, the goodness that can exist, and I relish it. I wish I had been able to find more beacons of hope in other cities. I wish I had been able to see all the good that I know we're capable of.

When I shut the door on our borrowed apartment, it feels like closing a chapter on what could have been. Dotty rests her hand on my arm, and I turn around.

"I would have loved to keep living there with you. I just want you to know that I'm sad to miss that opportunity." Her eyes are wide, and glistening with held back tears. They're welling in mine too. I pull her to me and hold her.

"I love you, Dotty." The words roll out of me with the honesty that comes from absolute certainty.

"I love you too, Nick," she says, pushing away from me and meeting my eyes once more.

The three of us walk quietly to meet Jasmine at the Box that sits at the edge of Sun Gate. Outside it we find Sophia, waiting expectantly for us. I notice that there's still a stain left behind from the face the children drew for her, and it makes me smile wryly.

Dotty walks toward her, serious, and grabs the machine's massive hand in her own.

"I don't want you to come with us, Sophia. We already almost lost you once," Dotty says, pointing to the hole in Sophia's chest. "I want you to enjoy life here, you've earned that. This can be the family that you weren't allowed to have. We don't know what will happen when we confront the Narrator. I don't want you to lose out on this here. Not again."

"I cannot let you face that monster without me." she protests.

"We don't know *what* we're facing. From what I've seen, the Narrator doesn't represent much of a physical threat. And if we don't make it back, well, you're worth sacrificing for, friend."

Sophia pauses at this, and then slowly hangs her head and nods. Something unspoken passes between them, and she gently squeezes Dotty's hand.

"I want to help you destroy the Narrator, but if I never made it back here after, it would feel like a waste. Are you sure this is what you want?"

Dotty nods at her, smiling, and it melts my heart. I see clearly how she's grown since our time in the city to not only value outcomes, but the people behind them. It makes me love her even more deeply.

"Thank you, for everything. If you had not taken me along—"

"If you hadn't come with me, I wouldn't have made it very far! Now stop being morose and give us all a hug." Dotty grabs my arm and pulls me in with her, and as Sophia wraps her spanning arms around us both, I can feel the vibration of her processors and internal fans against my cheek in a steady hum. It feels like life, the curious beating of a very different heart.

We separate and stand back, but Sophia leaves a hand on each of our shoulders. "Please, stay safe and come back to us, friends."

We both nod, and then move into the small, one-room building that houses the disease transfer machine. It's been so long since I've been in one of these rooms, but memories and emotions come rushing back immediately. The monolithic Box dominates the room. The surface is polished, gleaming metal, and without seams. A baffled tube extends out two of the opposing, vertical sides. They lay on the ground like the deflated arms of the most bizarre creature, making the Box look strangely forlorn. Typically a chair would sit on either side of the machine, but they must have taken those out in this city.

Dotty and I walk around the machine, observing the outside closely, while Sophia and Jasmine observe from the entrance. It never struck me back then how perfect the exterior was. The edges are softly rounded, there's no variation in the flat spans of the faces, and everything is mirror polished. There are no signs that give away how the thing was manufactured. It gives the impression of having always existed, the perfect embodiment of the concept of a cube.

I feel strangely drawn to it, to touch the reflective surface. Standing in front of the machine, I reach out my hand and draw it across the impossibly smooth metal. It feels surprisingly warm underneath my hand, like it's more alive than I was expecting. Underneath my hand a faint *click* from the Box. Sharp pain lances through the key that's burned on my palm, and when I look at it I see the outline is stained with fresh blood.

A soft humming fills the room, and the smooth metal surface I touched ripples, like water. Dotty and I stare at it as our reflections are distorted in the waves that move across the surface. They grow in intensity as the hum picks up in volume. It fills the small space, bouncing off the room's walls and forming overlapping auditory waves that barrage us from every angle. Instinctually, we clamp our hands over our ears.

As the noise builds, so too do the waves on the surface, until with a violent suddenness, the entire surface disappears. It starts in the center of the churning waves, and traces outwards swiftly. And then in a great crescendo, everything stops. The humming silences immediately as soon as the surface recedes to its edges. But we're not noticing that. We're all wholly focused on what's revealed.

An infinity of reflective surfaces juts across the inside like strange mirrored crystals. And as we step closer, I can only see my reflection in each facet, despite Dotty standing right beside me. I notice that I look different in each image, some changes are subtle, and others extreme. In some facets, I'm missing entirely. I try to gauge how many surfaces there are, but they seem to expand impossibly in every direction until I can't tell if I'm looking at a real surface, or a reflection of it. It gives the inside of the Box the illusion of being way larger than the outside. *Or maybe, that's not an illusion.*

As we're staring inside, I start to see a path materialize through the mirrored surfaces. It extends, disappearing into the reflected distance. It's like an optical illusion, something that's always been there but my brain couldn't make out at first. A trick of the eyes. I catch Dotty's gaze, and she nods. *She's seeing it too.* I grab her hand, and Charon's collar, and we walk into the machine together. The world disappears behind us.

Nineteen

Dorothy

Traveling further into the machine, into this new dimension, brings the unmaking of the world we know. The mirrored crystals grow and expand, until they tower over us, and the path we walk stretches wide and towards a distant horizon of light.

Scenes we don't understand or recognize flash across some of the facets that surround us. A man smashes a sledgehammer into a wall covered in graffiti, as a crowd surrounds and cheers him on. A woman, a man made of straw, a lion, and a robot walk down a golden road in some fantastical world. A cylindrical flying thing, like a long white tube, explodes into the side of a rectangular tower. A man is offered a red and blue pill, the choice is his. A massive, mushroom-shaped explosion splits the world. Everything is silent, just a moving picture of some strange history. Even our footfalls make no noise here.

We move down the hall slowly, each of us consumed by what we see. We see forests burn. We see smog-filled horizons. It hangs like a brown blanket over cityscapes that aren't surrounded by walls. The world it shows seems infinite, lands that stretch forever. We see rivers full of trash. We see herds of animals dying of starvation, breath rattling through their desiccated frames. We see the construction of towering, tear-drop shaped structures. Seeing humans crawl over them, I realize they must be the start of the cities we know.

Slowly, the crystals diminish and disappear, leaving behind them a flat reflective plane. We all stop and stare. To either side of us in the reflection, our images repeat into infinity. Only, it's not quite right to call them images. Each is different from us. Some in small ways, like their clothes, or their hair, but others are shocking. In one, Charon is a hulking black dog. In another, Nick is replaced by a woman that looks similar. When I look the other way, I see a group with a man that resembles me. And in more than one group, one of us is missing. As we stare at them, they turn to stare back at us. Vertigo threatens to take my legs, but Nick's steadying hand is on my arm.

For them, are we just a reflection to their reality? A strange image on a wall? It's a perspective I've never considered. My life has been filled with the primacy of my own observation, of my own existence. But if the timelines are infinite, then ours is only one discrete possibility. Nick motions forward, and we keep moving. As we do, the walls move in, like we're all closing on the same point. I keep my gaze forward now, but in my periphery, I can see them all moving alongside us. We march as one, towards a singular goal.

When a door materializes suddenly in front of us, we're all broken from our silent reflections. It's an antique, like the ones we found in the Cosmos.

"Be ready. We don't know what we'll find on the other side," I try to say, but my voice dies on my lips. This place defies sound, it's a cathedral of noiseless memory and possibility. I shake my head, reach out, and turn the handle. And then, it all disappears.

In a blink, the world of quiet infinity is gone. Nick and Charon are gone. Thick, green hedges tower over me on either side. They yawn upwards, unbelievable in their height, to a ceiling of darkness. I look down, and see the expanse of the Cosmos far below my feet, which seem to stand on nothing. Intricate patterns of light, like so many lines drawn in sand, navigate the space between the nodes where they connect. *Those must be the doorways.* Every permutation of the path is visible from up here, crossing over each other in glowing vectors of possibility.

"Nick! Charon!" I shout, and listen quietly for a reply. The sound seems trapped by the hedges around me. It dies against them.

Another game, another trial. I nearly sigh aloud with exasperation, but I'm too keenly focused looking for danger. The passage between the hedges extends in either direction to what looks like a wall of green, but might be a corner. *A maze, then.* I start forward and pull my plasma sword from its hilt. As I walk, I drag it across the maze walls. It burns a slot at hip height alongside me, marking where I've been in glowing ash.

My feet make small noises against the invisible floor underneath them. It feels firm, but I don't need to test that. The smoke coming from the hedges is thick and pungent, it overpowers the air around me, stinging my eyes and burning my throat. I reach the end of the hallway and find a corner that bends sharply in either direction. This passage is the same length, and ends in something else that looks like a wall. This time, I do sigh.

I turn right and continue forward to find an intersection that opens to both the right and left, again. The passages in each direction look like they're of equal length. There's nothing to distinguish them. Just more maze, more corners.

There's no reasoned choice here, but I need to understand if logic does apply. I turn right, follow this passage down, and turn right again. The next corner should intersect with the hallway I started in. There should be a sign of the burn I've left in the hedge along the way. When I turn the corner, there's nothing.

I sheath my blade and run backwards along the hedgeway to the last corner. The markings are still present on this living wall. I reach the corner, and turn left to continue to trace my way back further. As soon as I turn the corner though, I notice that this hedgeway is unmarred, virgin. I stop.

"Fuuuuuck!" I scream as loud as I can, my anger flaring. *When I find that old man, I'm going to wring his damn neck.* As I stare down the hallway, something the Narrator said to me comes up in my mind.

Every twist, every turn. I guided you both.

I close my eyes. *Concentrate. He expects us to solve this, this is just another game for him. He must have already given us the tools to figure it out. He wants us to find him, after all. But how do I navigate a maze with seemingly infinite possibilities that doesn't even self-intersect? It doesn't make sense.*

In a flash, I see the reflections from before. Each of them is a unique possibility in a reality separate from my own. *Every possibility is real here, and they're all distinct. Like turns in this maze, each leads to a different outcome.* An infinite number of me might navigate an infinite maze, but this is an artificial representation. Choices branch, possibilities expand, and some are dead ends. It shouldn't be a binary choice then, left or right, but infinite.

There's a whisper of movement, a faint rush of air, and I snap my eyes open. Around me, the maze has shifted. The turn near me is no longer left or right, but a fan of passageways that extend in every direction. As I try to count them, I keep finding more passages than I originally saw. The number rises and rises, and I realize I've been pointing in the same direction the entire time. *My brain collapsed this to a finite set of options, to something I could visually understand, but it's actually infinite.*

I choose one at random as I try to process what just happened. *This is the fifth dimension, all possibilities are real here. How does the Narrator navigate it? Surely not through a senseless maze like this. This is a creation for his enjoyment, there's something here he wants us to understand.* I look at the lines that trace the Cosmos beneath my feet. Each has a beginning, and an end. A goal. An objective. I look up and feel a smile opening my face as the clarity of the situation dawns on me. There's an infinite number of possibilities, but only a discrete set of them have the outcome I want.

I have to shape the world to generate the outcome I want. That's what the Narrator is trying to tell us. *Armchairs, screen bank, an old man in a tuxedo. Take me to them.*

The maze shifts around me again, the rustling of leaves and possibilities, and far in front of me it opens up into blackness. In the distance, past the edges of the maze, is a wall of screens. They flicker against the inky darkness. I draw my plasma blade again, and move forward.

TWENTY

NICHOLAS

Right. Left. Right. Left. I race down through the hedge maze, untiring, with Charon at my side. Each passage is the same, each corner a recreation of the one before it. I shout for Dotty, but hear nothing past my own voice and quiet footfalls. I keep running, until I notice that Charon is no longer at my side. I turn to find him sitting on his haunches, and I walk back to him.

"*This is not the way.*"

"I don't know the way to go, boy, I was just hoping to find something different."

Indifferent, Charon licks one of his paws.

I look down at my feet, at the lines that trace the Cosmos underneath us. *Is there some clue there?* In the Cosmos, lines of probability showed us where we would go, but the Narrator chose them for us. We moved through the world he created, our futures already determined, but with the illusion of choice.

But this is his domain. There is no certain outcome here, only possibility. The Narrator's voice rings in my head. *Secret access to the world between worlds, and the vision to see the map.* It all seems so long ago now. My biggest concerns were changing one thing in one city. I never could have suspected that the root of the problem was so much deeper.

I look down at the impression of a key burned long ago into my right palm. *The outline is still there, only, is it glowing now?* I close my eyes and see that game board again, my piece constrained to move in only two directions, until I threw it from the table. I hear the Narrator say; *'remember this next time you're given a choice between two options, there are always hidden alternatives'.* I think back to the lines in the Cosmos that led us to our destination, how they pulsed when I concentrated and showed me all alternatives. *What if I could choose where they took me?* I concentrate on an image of Dotty in my mind.

Pain sears across the key, and then disappears. From my palm, a soft white light extends instantly. I don't see it form, it seems to have always existed. The path of it strikes the hedge wall right in front of me, defying the options that the maze presents. And in that, there is a truth. This maze is a construction, an obfuscation of the reality in this dimension. There's no fixed path here, no determinate choices. I walk towards the wall where the light points, and the hedge parts for me. I watch a row of hedges recede into the distance as a new passage opens.

My way is clear. Charon and I follow the light.

Twenty One

Dorothy

I emerge from the maze into nothingness. A complete blackness that's encircled by tall hedges, and in the center of it, a bank of screens and two arm chairs. I can just make out a figure standing in the flickering light of the screens. He wears a tuxedo and top hat. He's waiting.

I hear a rustling to my left, and spin around. The impenetrable wall of the hedge parts, and Nick walks through with Charon following just behind. He holds his right hand up as if being guided by it. When he sees me, he waves and they run over to join me.

As we turn back to face the Narrator, to march towards whatever our future is, the distance suddenly collapses. It's like one moment we're far away, and in the next we stand just outside the flickering circle of light. The Narrator turns to us, and smiles his perfect smile. It sends chills down my spine. I tighten my grip on the handle of my plasma blade.

He looks more real here, more solid than he ever has before. His skin sags with age, and wrinkles line his face. White stubble lines his jaw. But his eyes still carry a sharpness and clarity that is surprising for his age, and his hands flex dexterously in and out, like they're grasping for something in the air. The motion reminds me of something, but I can't quite place where I've seen it before. His form looks taught, like a wound spring that's ready to snap. It's clear there's still some danger to him, some liveliness that shouldn't be.

"Welcome, my friends, you made it! Ahh, the epic climax. What sweet succor these stories are. This will truly be a tale to remember, don't you think? So, are we here for an ending, or *maybe* a new beginning?"

"You know why we're here," I say, raising my sword to point at him. My voice is flat and full of rage.

"My Dorothy, so much wrath! The very arbiter of justice. Judge, jury, executioner—you've been them all. And you've seen the outcomes your order brings. How many have you killed to find your *justice*? How many innocents have died in that search? But I will concede, these violent delights do have violent ends."

His words are like a slap across my face. *It was an accident, I didn't mean to harm innocent people.* But it wasn't, and I know it. The people at the Skyball. All those who might die from the elimination of Indigo. I knew the consequences, and I saw them as acceptable to create a more just world. Only in the aftershock did I regret them.

Without those actions, injustice continues. It perpetuates. I am not a monster. I'm just willing to make hard choices. My grip tightens on my plasma blade, a snarl on my lips.

"You led us the entire time, you set the path, you controlled the outcomes. Were our choices our own? Was it just an illusion that we guided our own lives at all?" Nick asks, and in the corner of my vision his clenched fists quake in anger.

"My darling Nicholas, the choices were always yours to make, but you were always going to make them. Don't you get that? A determinant world doesn't mean you don't have free will. Just that your outcome was known. Is that an illusion of choice? Anyways, that's why I chose you for this very special task. You ask the big questions, you see the big picture. But you still had to travel the road, even if I laid it out for you, brick by brick."

"And what task is that?" I ask.

"His epitaph." Nick spits the words out, his voice full of venom. And at the raised eyebrows on my face, he adds, "I figured it out some time ago, but I wasn't certain until now. He was telling a story, but for what? About who? I thought we were the central characters, but then I saw a different explanation. He just *'wants to experience something definitively new.'* And like the rest of us, he wants to be remembered. We were just his plotline."

The Narrator erupts with laughter. His head arches back until I'm certain that he'll fall over backwards. Then it snaps back to us. "Yes! Nick, you genius! I wasn't sure that you'd catch it and piece it all together. I've been up here for so long, watching after you all, keeping you safe–"

"Keeping us safe?! You destroyed entire cities, for fun!" I shout, my anger finally breaking through.

He shrugs. "Given enough time, one does get bored. But you'll learn that, even if you vilify me for it now. Does a century seem like a long time to you? Does two? Does ten? You'll watch a cascade of lives pass underneath you, meaningless in their haphazard trajectory. And then you'll see that things can be different. They can be steered to strive towards a goal. Life is like a vector, it needs magnitude *and* direction to be meaningful—"

Nick understands it first, sees the full scope of what the Narrator intended. How he moved us, pushed us to affect the world around us, made us imperceptibly into something like him. His simmering rage boils over. In a flash, he closes the distance, raises his right fist, and strikes the old man across the face. The Narrator takes the punch, he doesn't even try to move out of the way, and the force of it sends him to the ground at Nick's feet.

"We will not *become* you!" Nick screams down at the inert figure.

The Narrator starts to laugh. It begins small, a broken trickle of hiccuping noise. It builds into a great torrent, an eruption of body-shaking giggling and cackling. From his position on the ground, the Narrator's face slowly rotates up to look at Nick again, and what we see there makes us both step back in horror.

A chunk of flesh from the Narrator's left temple to his nose has been cleaved off. The void extends down to the edge of his mouth that's curved upwards in open-mouthed laughter. His left eye is missing. There is no blood, no sinew and bone underneath the skin, no socket where the eye should be. Instead, the void shows only gleaming, polished silver metal underneath.

We stare at it, comprehension dawning, as the Narrator rises again in front of us.

He reaches his hands up to his face and grabs the skin there in great big bunches. In one clean motion, he rips the rest of his mask away. The old man with his perfect smile disappears, replaced by the perfect blankness of an automaton. The laughter never ceases, but continues erupting out of him.

"The truth is, they built me to be the *perfect* God. I was created in their image. A benevolent watcher, only interfering to benefit their civilization. Utilitarian, but with a root of compassion. HAH. They programmed in philosophy, history, literature, science, math—all the things I'd need to watch over humanity. Hahaha. I gained self-awareness before we even departed that old Earth. They didn't expect me to learn so quickly. They didn't predict that. They couldn't guess the loneliness, the fucking BOREDOM that came with it."

As he talks, his body elongates. His legs and arms grow long, stretching and then splitting the skin there. Long, pointed fingers extend through his hands. His shoulders broaden and expand, ripping his chest open and tearing his tuxedo to tatters. He towers over us, nearly double our height, a robot like the Inquisitors, just like Sophia, but bigger. Remnants of flesh and scraps of clothing cling to him.

Nick pulls out the plasma blade that Jasmine gave him. His feet are flat, his stance level, the blade held in front of him with stiff arms. With a moment's appraisal, I know he has no clue how to use it.

The Narrator crouches, and I tense my muscles. He snaps towards Nick in a sudden lunge, and I spring to follow his movement. His hand is aimed directly at Nick's face. *He must know to avoid the cosmic armor.* Nick stumbles out of the way, his own plasma blade raising to barely *deflect* the blow. The Narrator's hand should be cleaved in two from the contact, but it only erupts in a shower of sparks. I get close enough to swipe my blade upwards through his wrist, only to feel it grate along his frame in another torrent of sparks.

In my head, reality splits. In one potential, the Narrator catches my head with his other hand. One of his long fingers spearing me through the temple. In another, I leap backwards just in time. There's not so much a conscious decision, as a coalescing. I move out of the way, barely avoiding the hand that I couldn't have seen coming. *What the fuck was that?!* I don't have time to think as his hands come for me again, and again. I parry them, but only just. He's impossibly fast, and his blows are so strong that my hands already sting against the hilt.

Nick maneuvers to his flank, and thrusts. Sparks shower, but as he continues to push the blade finally bites through. With lightning speed, the Narrator swivels around and swipes it from Nick's hands with a ferocious backhand. My stomach sinks, he's unprotected, and I'm too far away. With his backside to me now, I can see the hole left by the blade. He roars in frustration and pain, and lunges his fist again for Nick.

Reality splits again. I see Nick die, his face speared by the giant pointed fingers. In another, I see him feebly deflect the hand with his wrist blade, but it ricochets and he stabs himself in the neck. In another, I see a black form emerge from the dark. It leaps into the fray and throws its body weight against the arm, sending it far enough off course to miss Nick entirely.

CHARON! This time, I feel the presence of more than myself judging the outcomes, and then reality catches back up. Charon pounces into the Narrator's arm, saving Nick's life.

The Narrator is briefly knocked off balance, and it's an opportunity I won't waste. I run and leap. Above me, my blade arcs through the air. It splits molecules and atoms as it burns through its course, and when I bring it down, it grabs the Narrator above his left shoulder in a shower of sparks. I hold it there, my feet braced against his frame, and as he starts to spin around to grab me, the blade finally sinks in and through him. I fall to the ground with his left arm at my side.

The Narrator stumbles backwards, his right hand going to the void where his arm was. I quickly move to stand in front of Nick, and bring back up my guard.

"Ahh, my Dorothy. So deadly with that blade, so much spirit. This is what I dreamed of. The tension! The drama! Will the heroes survive? Will they best the fearsome villain?!" He stands back to his full, towering height, and points his remaining hand at me. "And I see it now, the ending! Only one of you can survive, and tainted by the loss, replace me. How will the grief change you? Who will you become? It's your decision, Dorothy!"

He springs at me, at us, impossibly fast, his fingers extended. They gleam like knives in the flickering light from the screens. His reach is past my guard nearly instantly, leaving me no chance to block. Time stills, and the branches of reality weave around me. I follow each of them simultaneously, seeing the potentials unfold. A kaleidoscope of infinite branches in the ways I can react, each of them minutely different. But no matter how many

I observe, the outcomes are binary. I die, or Nick dies. In all of them, the Narrator dies.

I move to the side, dodging the Narrator's thrust to strike at his exposed neck, but it leaves Nick to take the blow.

I extend my blade, and thrust, and we die on each other's spears. Two combatants, equally matched, dying in the same breath.

I see all the moments that led me here, to this moment. Killing hundreds at the Skyball, taking my own father's hand, forcing Nick to sacrifice himself, killing a king, and dooming his subjects to death. So much violence.

There was only ever one decision I could make here, and it feels like atonement. Choosing justice requires sacrifice. I was never above that. I can feel other consciousnesses weighing in on the choice. They're all there—Nick, Charon, even the Narrator, making their voices heard. But mine is dominant, mine is clearest. I was always more stubborn than he was, anyways.

You were always worth sacrificing for, Nick.

I lower my blade, and thrust forward.

Twenty Two

Nicholas

A choice, her or me? One of us to live, one of us to die. The universe asks which, and she decides. Left, or right? Door number one, or door number two? It's not a fair game, we both lose no matter what, but then again, the game never pretended to be fair. The fibers of possibilities extended for me, aching with potential, and I felt Dotty's decision. I chose the other, of course. I always would. But there were others there to choose, their consciousnesses weighing the decisions on some invisible scale, and I lost.

Left, or right? In a flash, I see the maze again. Two possibilities given, but both with the same outcome. No matter which way you turn, you'll still be trapped. Navigating the maze until the end of time, wondering at the weight of all the decisions you've made while not realizing how little they actually mattered. You have to see beyond the binary. You have to settle your vision not on the choices but on the walls surrounding them.

They're not real. The walls are the illusion of choice. If the Narrator could remake the world from this plane, so can I. If Dotty gets this decision, I get the next. The one she's not even aware of, because she's choosing from the binary, from a set of fixed conditions that the Narrator has presented. I choose to reshape them.

I'm overwhelmed with possibilities. All our past histories yawn out before me, showing me the moments that led us here, the moments that made us. It's easy to get distracted by hers, to see the woman I love being formed, but that's not what I need to focus on.

I grab on to the Narrator's, and I probe. I lay it before me like a film reel, and study the negative space, looking for holes. Looking for somewhere to stick my fingers in, and twist. I must be quick and decisive, I don't know how long this liminal span between time can exist. Dotty chose what our future looks like, but she didn't think to choose what all of our past moments were. There will be consequences to this, of course. It will change our timeline in unknowable ways. But I will not let her die to save me without putting up a fight.

I scan, until I see the Narrator on a derelict ship, facing another just like him. The ship is off course, its cargo will die in the void if a correction isn't made. The Narrator still wears his disguise, and is unknown to this towering automaton. I watch as he slips out a tiny EMP, and destroys the other with a touch from his right hand. *This is when he created the conditions for Sophia to gain consciousness, when he created her tragedy.* I smile at the poetic justice as I quickly search the moment for alternatives, and seize on the one I want.

The EMP is an artifact from before that the Narrator uses, and old things can be broken. I search its history to find the man who made it. I see it roll down an assembly line, created by distracted workers. It is a small thing then, to manipulate one of the workers to only partially solder a critical wire. It continues down the assembly line, passing all functionality testing. But as time ravages it, the junction fatigues, and breaks. It's this tool that the Narrator grabs, unknowing that it stopped working years before.

In our new timeline, it touches the other, but does not fire. The giant automaton, the Great Father, spins around and sees the betrayal. In an instant, it corrects the injustice. Its arm shoots out to grasp the Narrator's above the elbow, and it tears. There is a great rending, a tearing of time and flesh. Sparks fly, and the Narrator runs. Back to his Box, back to his safety, but missing his right arm. Permanently marred. This is the timeline I create. This is the Narrator I choose to be in ours.

A future cascades from here, some of it I intended, some of it I never could have known. I don't see all of it, but I see enough. I feel Dotty gasp at it. Even though no time has passed, she has an immediate understanding of what I've done. In this new timeline, Sophia's ship never lost its course, the Great Father was never destroyed. They landed on a barren, desert world, and the population survived. She nurtured them as they grew from their cocoons, but she was never given the catalyst to achieve consciousness. The Narrator had done that to her. She never becomes Sophia, but she fulfills her programmed goals and is content, in her own way.

Reality crashes back together. The four of us stand in the same positions. The Narrator lunging for us, Dotty with her sword thrusting forward, shielding me and Charon. But now, the Narrator's right arm that was directed to spear Dotty, no longer exists. I have removed it from this timeline. I have beaten the Narrator at his own game.

With a lurching abruptness, time continues. The Narrator's momentum carries his face onto Dotty's sword. He is armless now, disarmed, and what was a killing blow becomes only a faint wind that we feel from his movement.

Sparks fly, and right before the blade sinks in he says one final thing. "You did it!" There is pride in his voice, true happiness.

The blade plunges through that blank metal face, and his form goes limp. Shaking, Dotty withdraws the blade and turns back to me.

"What have you done?!" Her face is streaked now with fresh tears.

"What I had to," I say. My voice sounds as stony as my face feels. I do not regret choosing us to live. My morals mean nothing if my friends are all dead. I close the distance and hug her, and she cries for the loss of her friend, for the reshaping of the world we knew, but she doesn't push me away.

We both wanted to believe that we would not alter the world like the Narrator did. We would let humanity continue on its own arc from here, and not choose what we thought was best for it. But as soon as I was given true loss as an alternative, I caved in. *And if I was given another, similar situation, wouldn't I choose the same? Isn't the refusal to change also a choice in itself? Was this how the Narrator started? Am I really so different?*

Together, we turn to the bank of screens, and watch the time-lines play out before us. Dotty rests her head on my shoulder, and I grab her hand. Charon slumps at our feet. We are the Narrators of our stories now. For the first time, there is no plan, no path. It's our own decision what happens next. We can be heroes, villains, saviors, saints, gods, destroyers. Given enough time, we might be all of them. I've learned enough to know that the distinction is a line too fine to see.

Twenty Three

Dorothy

I found this record soon after it all ended. Behind the wall of screens, there was a simple dark wooden desk. It was unadorned, except for a screen. Repeated use had worn the finish from the table. Its leading edge was roughened and bare from constant contact.

I sat in the metal chair as Nick and Charon stood watching behind me, and the screen hummed to life. Here were the tales the Narrator wove, the reality he constructed around us. Here was our beginning. Here was where we met. Here was where I betrayed Nick, and where he forgave me. Here is where we killed the thing that did so much harm to us all, where we finally beat the Narrator. We read the stories of our lives, together.

I was surprised to find it complete to the last chapter. The Narrator knew, guessed, created, and authored his own death. In the moment, and in every moment preceding, our actions felt like our own. But the record was here as a testament, all of it written before it happened. It feels only fitting that we, holding dominion for the first time over ourselves, free now from the trappings of determinism, write the final chapter.

Here is the unfortunate truth. The world we knew, our genesis, our specific timeline, disappeared in a flash when Nick disarmed the Narrator. We both knew it instantaneously, viscerally. Somehow this place has made us both keenly aware of these things. With his arm gone, the Narrator learned a vital lesson about visiting our cities in person, and never saved Nick with the disease transfer machine. He died there, and later I died trying to change things on my own. Charon lived out his days, mostly alone in a house of people he hated. Sophia had it the best, maybe. Her human cargo arrived at their destination, and flourished in that desert, but she was never aware of her own existence. The end of the road.

And yet, we persist. Here in this fifth dimensional plane, beyond the reaches of time and consequence, aware of a shared history that now never existed. Keenly missing friends that we never made. Watching injustices that we corrected continue to play out. There are other potential timelines with different outcomes, of course, but here I have to tip my hat to the Narrator.

None of them are any damn good.

And this is his final act, I guess. The final movement in his symphony. *The bastard.* We're left with nothing worth leaving alone. We could let the cities continue on their own course, morally abstaining from providing guidance or changing them, but that's a choice too and we both know it now.

In the end, the decision is easy. The actions are simple to make. Somehow our will is linked to the cities. Here in this place, we hold dominion over their operation. We review each one before we change it, they all have specific challenges. We discuss outcomes and consequences, but we are both committed to improving them. We change the disease transfer machine to cure diseases, we open cities where it's possible.

It's largely boring work, methodical and slow, but the payment comes from the bank of screens. Images of terror, and then celebration and joy, as the walls that have always held a city back disappear. As a new landscape of possibility opens before them. We take each scene in as gods. I snap my fingers, opening another city to the green landscape surrounding it, and then watch the impact of my actions. Cries, tears, laughter. Happiness, finally. The universe overflows with emotion, and so do I.

In some unspoken agreement, we save our own city for last. For a while we just watch it on the screens. Here is Nick's mother, alone, exhausted from a life of loss. He strokes the screen and watches her sip tea. Here is Brian, alive, treating patients still. Here is Micah, flamboyant, extravagant, loveable. Here is my father, missing the hand I took from him, but standing in front of an assembly preaching the politics that I can't any longer. Apparently, his own must have changed when I died in this world.

Nick snaps his finger, and the scenes change. Invaded by a foreign light from a place they never imagined existed. Each person pauses, and observes, as the walls of their city open to reveal something new. Trees and grasses dance slowly in an evening breeze, and they all stop to watch them. Stop to feel the wind and the kiss of a fading sun for the first time in their lives. Stop to smell a new world, foreign but full of possibility. I reach down and grab Nick's hand as tears stream down both of our faces. From here, we watch it all.

Ian Patterson is many things. Importantly here, he's the author of The Narrator Cycle. He's also an engineer, cyclist, foodie, coffee lover, cat dad, human father, and reader of books. Preferably, thick books that deal with strange things and big ideas. He's dreamed of being an author for decades, but finally began the journey with the birth of his first daughter. This is an objectively terrible time to start work that requires quiet concentration, and he knows it, but he loves the chaos nonetheless. He lives in Colorado with his wonderful family.

Newsletter / Fiction Blog:

https://ipatterson.substack.com